# *FROM THE NANCY DREW FILES*

*THE CASE: While on a romantic cruise to Rio, Nancy gets involved in a bizarre treasure hunt for a cache of hot gems.*

*CONTACT:* Captain John Brant *invites* Carson Drew *and* Nancy *on a vacation that becomes serious business.*

*SUSPECTS:* Nina da Silva—*the beautiful widow is out to steal Carson Drew's heart—or maybe a fortune in hidden gems.*

Antonio Ribeira—*the tall, dark crew member is too smooth for his own good—or anyone else's.*

Lynn Ashley—*is the Southern belle trying to snare a husband—or to outfox Nancy?*

*COMPLICATIONS: The very handsome assistant cruise director is making a big play for Nancy—and Ned is due at the next port!*

Books in The Nancy Drew™ Series

No. 21 RECIPE FOR MURDER
No. 22 FATAL ATTRACTION
No. 23 SINISTER PARADISE
No. 24 TILL DEATH DO US PART
No. 25 RICH AND DANGEROUS
No. 26 PLAYING WITH FIRE
No. 27 MOST LIKELY TO DIE
No. 28 THE BLACK WIDOW

# THE BLACK WIDOW

Carolyn Keene

AN ARCHWAY PAPERBACK
Published by SIMON & SCHUSTER
New York London Toronto Sydney Tokyo Singapore

This book is a work of fiction. Names, characters, places and incidents are either the product of the author's imagination or are used fictitiously. Any resemblance to actual events or locales or persons, living or dead, is entirely coincidental.

An Archway paperback
first published in Great Britain
by Simon & Schuster Ltd in 1992
A Paramount Communications Company



**Simon & Schuster Ltd**
**West Garden Place**
**Kendal Street**
**London W2 2AQ**



Simon & Schuster of Australia Pty Ltd
Sydney

A CIP catalogue record for this book is
available from the British Library

ISBN 0-671-71644-1

Printed and bound in Great Britain by
HarperCollins *Manufacturing*

# THE BLACK WIDOW

# Chapter One

"LOOK OUT! YOU'RE going to kill that guy!"

Nancy Drew braced her long legs against the limousine's floor, gripping the edge of the leather seat. Her blue eyes widened as the limo careered wildly down a narrow street in Buenos Aires, Argentina, narrowly missing a well-dressed elderly pedestrian. She could hear his shouts fading rapidly behind them an instant later.

The chauffeur turned around in his seat and smiled broadly at Nancy. "Have no fear, senorita!" he said, waving both hands for emphasis. The limousine swerved, almost mowing down a group of black-clad nuns.

"Be careful! *Cuidado!*" shouted Nancy's father, Carson Drew. The driver nodded and twisted the wheel sharply to the right. They turned a corner on two wheels, and Carson Drew sank back into his seat, mopping his brow.

The Drews were on their way from the airport to Mirabella Pier in Buenos Aires, Argentina. Carson's old friend Captain John Brant had invited them down for a few days on the cruise liner he now commanded. He'd arranged for a driver, so the Drews could ride to the harbor in style, but Nancy wasn't sure they'd get there at all.

The driver abruptly slammed on the brakes. "*Plaza de Mayo. Tráfico.* Is very bad," he grumbled, gesturing at the sudden snarl of traffic outside. The car began to move forward again at a slow crawl. Nancy relaxed and looked out the tinted window.

An enormous stone cathedral loomed against the brilliant sky. Businessmen in pinstriped suits and elegant afternoon shoppers thronged the square, brushing shoulders with vendors in multicolored cotton ponchos. The summer sun shimmered on the paving stones, drenching faces with reflected light.

Nancy sighed happily. "This is more like it," she said. "*Now* I can't wait to get on with our vacation and meet Captain Brant," Nancy said. "Although I guess he won't have much time to socialize. I mean, the *Emerald Queen* is the fleet's flagship, right?"

"That's right," Carson replied. "But if I know John, he'll find time for us." He shook his head in wonder. "We haven't seen each other since before you were born—that makes it at least eighteen years. After John went into the Merchant Marines and my practice got going, we never seemed to be in the same place at the same time. But we have always kept in touch."

"He had a fabulous idea for a reunion," Nancy said. "I'm ready for sunshine and ocean breezes."

She pushed her reddish gold hair back from her face. "Can I take another look at our route?"

Carson pulled out the glossy cruise brochure and handed it to his daughter. "Perfect," Nancy murmured as she reread the itinerary. "A few days at sea, a couple of stops, and then we end up in Rio de Janeiro, just in time for Carnival."

"Mmmm. It does sound good," her father agreed.

"I've heard Carnival is even wilder than Mardi Gras in New Orleans," Nancy said. "Ned is looking forward to the costume parties. I don't think he's ever outgrown Halloween!" Ned Nickerson, Nancy's longtime boyfriend, was planning to meet the Drews in Rio for the week of Carnival. Nancy could hardly wait. Romantic

Rio with the guy she loved—what could be better?

The limo began to pull into the pierside parking area. Nancy leaned forward. Ahead, the huge luxury liners lay in their berths. "Which one do you think is the *Emerald Queen?"* she asked her father.

Carson Drew shot an amused glance at his daughter. "Some detective," he said, teasing her. "I'd say it's got to be that one there—the one with all the *emerald green* streamers."

"This detective is on vacation, remember?" Nancy protested, but then had to laugh at herself.

As they got out of the limo, a warm, moist, salty breeze ruffled Nancy's hair. A large, cheerful-looking man in a crisp white uniform came striding toward them. His red face and twinkling eyes stood out in contrast to Carson's grave, distinguished features. And while Carson's hair had silvered with the years, this man's thatch of close-cropped dark curls seemed untouched by time. He seized Carson's hand and shook it vigorously.

"Carson!" he exclaimed. "I can't believe I finally got you down here!"

"John, you old seadog! You look exactly the same. You've added a few bars to your uniform, I notice."

"Yes, and a few inches around the middle,

too—must be the great food I've heard about on these cruise liners." The captain turned to Nancy and took her hands in his beefy ones. "And you must be Nancy. Did you know that your father *mailed* me a cigar when you were born?"

Nancy laughed. "Dad always does things with flair," she said.

"Carson tells me you've become something of a celebrity. You're a detective, if I'm not mistaken. Very impressive. Carson has every reason to be proud of you."

"Thanks." Nancy blushed, a little embarrassed by Captain Brant's praise. She was glad when they arrived at the gangplank, where an attractive dark-haired woman of about thirty-five was climbing out of a white limo. Two porters had already begun to load her luggage onto a trolley. The captain gestured in her direction.

"There's my other special guest," he said with a warm smile for the woman. "Nina da Silva, I'd like you to meet my old friend Carson Drew and his daughter, Nancy. Nina's late husband, Hector, was a colleague of mine," he explained to the Drews.

As Nancy shook hands with Nina da Silva, she took in the woman's elegant black linen suit, accented by a beautiful emerald necklace in an antique setting. She also noticed the tiny vertical lines of worry between Nina's long-lashed dark eyes—and the tight set of her slim shoulders.

A porter let one of her suitcases slip off the trolley, and she jumped visibly as it crashed to the dock.

"Be careful with that," she snapped irritably. Nancy was surprised at the woman's reaction. Nina da Silva seemed tense and preoccupied. I wonder why? Nancy thought and then smiled at herself. Come on, Drew, she scolded mentally. This is a vacation—don't forget!

The porters moved up the gangplank with the luggage trolleys, the Drews, Captain Brant, and Nina da Silva following. "I hope this cruise won't be too tame for you, Nancy," the captain said. "After all, the biggest mystery on this ship is what the chef puts in his secret soufflé." He turned back to Nina. "Nancy here is a private eye," he explained. "And Carson's a famous criminal lawyer. Quite a family, eh?"

Nancy grinned. Captain Brant's enthusiasm was infectious.

Nina's eyes widened. "Really! How interesting," she said. She turned to look closely at Nancy. "That must be fascinating work."

She lurched suddenly, her foot slipping on the gangplank. Carson quickly grabbed her elbow to steady her. "Careful, or we'll have a 'man' overboard before we even sail!" he cautioned.

Nancy noticed the concern in her father's voice and the way his hand lingered on Nina's arm, even after she was safely on deck. Their eyes met and held as Nina smiled her thanks. Nancy was surprised to feel a tiny stab of envy.

"Let's see now," Captain Brant said, consulting a computer printout handed to him just then. "You're all on the Opal Deck. Nina, you and Carson are practically next-door neighbors. Nancy, you're just around the corner and down the alleyway—that's the hall, to you landlubbers.

"The Opal's the best deck on the ship. It's up high enough so you get a wonderful view, but it's still far enough below the Emerald Deck so you won't get any of the noise."

"This ship is huge!" Nancy said, looking around. "It's like a gigantic hotel—only it floats. How many decks are there?"

"Eight," replied the captain proudly. "The Emerald Deck is on top—that's the glassed-in one with the formal dining room and the Emerald Ballroom. Most of the passengers' cabins and the athletic facilities are on the next three. Then there's the Amethyst Deck, where there are a few more cabins and also officers' quarters.

"The main deck, just below the Amethyst, is sort of like a hotel lobby, with a florist, a gift shop, and a few other shops. All lifeboats and crew quarters are on the two lower decks. There'll be a tour and a lifeboat drill before dinner, so you can see for yourselves."

"Sounds impressive! But right now I could use a shower and a change of clothes," Nancy said.

She looked down at her bulky sweater and black jeans. "It's still winter in the northern hemisphere, you know."

"Yes, it's been a long trip," her father put in.

"Fine, fine. Julio here will show you to your cabins," the captain replied. He looked at his watch. "The tours are staggered—yours starts at five-thirty. That gives you forty-five minutes to get tropical."

"Tall order, Captain," Carson said, grinning at his friend.

Brant clapped Carson on the shoulder, returning the grin. "KP duty if you're not wearing an aloha shirt next time I see you, Drew," he threatened. Nancy giggled.

"I'd like you all to join me for dinner this evening," the captain said. He strode away, and the three passengers followed the porter up to the Opal Deck.

Nancy's cabin was large and luxurious. A thick cream-colored carpet covered the floor, and the bed was hidden under an apricot satin quilt and mounds of matching pillows. Nancy threw her winter coat over a chair and looked around appreciatively. This is traveling in style! she thought.

She caught sight of a brown paper package that lay on the dressing table, next to a crystal vase full of white roses. The typed label said, "To Ms. Nancy Drew, detective. From her fans in River Heights."

Nancy tore open the package and began to laugh. She pulled out a black bikini. Bess Marvin and George Fayne, her two best friends, were at it again! Last week they had helped Nancy shop for a cruise wardrobe. Blond, flirtatious Bess had tried to convince Nancy to buy the almost nonexistent bikini. Nancy smiled now, remembering.

"Oh, come on, Nan, it looks fantastic on you! If only it looked that way on *me,"* Bess had said wistfully. "Come on, buy it!"

"Are you kidding, Bess?" said George. "I seriously doubt Nan's dad would approve."

"George does have a point," Nancy said to Bess.

"Oh, well," Bess said. "You'd probably get a sunburned stomach, anyway." But there had been an unmistakable gleam in her blue eyes as she put the suit back on the rack.

Well, now we'll see how open-minded Dad is, Nancy thought as she started to unpack a strapless silk sheath dress. Its deep blue color set off her eyes dramatically. Definitely sizzling, Nancy thought as she took it out of its wrapping.

As Nancy hung the gown in her closet, she heard a slight rustling noise behind her. Turning, she saw a white envelope lying on the carpet in front of the door. "I *know* that wasn't there earlier," she said aloud.

She ran to the door, threw it open, and looked up and down the hall. No one.

She picked up the envelope and tore it open.

As she pulled out a piece of folded paper, a smaller scrap fluttered to the floor.

Nancy unfolded the first piece of paper. It was a crude drawing of a red-eyed spider, with a red hourglass on its belly. A black widow spider.

At the ends of its eight hairy legs were faint penciled marks. Nancy squinted at them. They were actually tiny letters. They seemed to be chosen at random: *A, W, N, P, I, Y, N,* and *F,* if she read clockwise. Nancy repeated the letters to herself.

She picked up the scrap of paper from the carpet. It was a scrawled note. It said:

The black widow is the key.
Time is running out!

Is this for real? Nancy wondered. Or are Bess and George trying to spice up my vacation with this old-fashioned code stuff? But how could they pull a stunt like this, long-distance?

Let's see what Dad makes of this, she decided. He's great at puzzles.

Nancy locked her door and started toward her father's cabin. As she turned the corner, she saw him down the hall, knocking at a door.

I'll bet that's Mrs. da Silva's cabin, Nancy thought. Am I going to be a fifth wheel right now? She stopped walking, suddenly unsure of herself.

At that moment a scream ripped through the air. Nancy sprinted forward. Carson Drew flung open Mrs. da Silva's door, and Nancy ran in right behind him.

Nina da Silva lay on the floor. She was very pale. Carson fell to his knees beside her. She didn't stir as he took her wrist and felt for a pulse.

Nancy's eyes flew to the dresser. Something was moving there.

She stepped closer. On the dresser was a fancy box of chocolates with the lid half off. As she watched, the cover shifted even more and slid onto the dresser top.

A slender black thread looped itself over the side of the box. Then another. A round black body appeared, with a splash of red.

It was a black widow spider!

# Chapter Two

"DAD—LOOK!"

As Nancy peered into the box, her skin crawled. It was a nightmare come true. The box was seething with spiders, dozens of them climbing sluggishly over one another. Behind her, Carson drew in a sharp breath.

She scanned the room quickly, spotting the porthole just to the left of the dressing table. Edging past the box, she yanked open the porthole latch. Then she ran to the bathroom and grabbed the thickest towel.

"Nancy! What are you doing?" Carson started toward her, but Nancy stopped him.

"They'll be all over the cabin if I don't get rid of them," she said grimly. "This towel should protect me in case they're feeling hungry."

She closed her eyes for a second, gathering her courage. Then, gritting her teeth, she scooped up the box, spiders and all, and hurled it into the ocean.

"Ugh! What a relief," Nancy said. She rubbed her hands on the legs of her black jeans, trying to erase the creepy feeling. Then she turned to her father, who was kneeling once again beside the motionless figure of Nina da Silva.

"Let's get her up onto the bed," Carson said anxiously. "She's out cold, but I don't think she's hurt. There are no bites on her hands or face. I doubt she'll want to wake up lying on the floor, though."

Nancy and Carson lifted Mrs. da Silva and gently maneuvered her onto the bed.

"Are you sure you're okay, Nancy?" asked Carson worriedly.

"Yes," replied Nancy. "A little shaky, but unbitten." She went into the bathroom and got a glass of water. Carson took it from her and sprinkled some on Nina da Silva's forehead.

Nancy bit her lip thoughtfully. "Dad, I wonder if this spider thing is a coincidence or something else," she said. "I was just coming to show you a note someone put under my door."

Her father took the note and drawing. "Looks like some prankster's idea of a joke," he commented.

Nancy shook her head doubtfully. "I don't know. Those spiders were no joke. All Mrs. da Silva had to do was reach for a chocolate, and—" She shuddered at the thought.

Nina da Silva sighed just then, and her eyelids fluttered open. Carson leaned forward. "How are you feeling?"

The woman smiled weakly. "I've felt better."

"Did any of the spiders bite you?" Carson asked intently.

"The spiders? No—" Nina's eyes darkened at the memory. Then she seemed to snap out of it and struggled to a sitting position.

"Mrs. da Silva," Nancy said carefully, "do you have any idea where that box came from? Or who might have sent it?"

Nina da Silva shook her head. "It must have been a practical joke of some kind. When a woman travels alone in this country she attracts attention."

"However, I think it is best forgotten. There's really no point in troubling Captain Brant about such a trifle, unpleasant though it might be. Don't you agree?" She got shakily to her feet. "I believe we have an obligation to be present at the drill in a few minutes. And I still have some unpacking to do. Thank you again for your trouble."

Nancy and her father knew a dismissal when they heard it, however politely it was put.

They turned to leave. "Well," Carson Drew said with a puzzled shake of his head, "I guess we'll get moving, if you're sure you're all right."

Nancy looked at her watch. It was five-fifteen. "Oh, no! I haven't even taken a shower yet! See you on deck," she called as she dashed back to her cabin.

She showered with lightning speed, threw on a white cotton sundress and new sandals, and hurried to the fore end of the deck, dabbing on lip gloss as she ran. She was still moving at top speed when she rounded a corner and collided head-on with another moving body.

"Oh, excuse me—I'm really sorry," Nancy gasped. She tried to stifle a guilty giggle.

The girl she had bumped into didn't think it was funny at all. She was about Nancy's height, an ash blonde in a tight jumpsuit. She was pretty in an artificial way.

She glared at Nancy, her blue eyes sharp as daggers. "Listen, honey, maybe you need to go back to charm school and learn to look where you're going," she spat out and flounced off toward the waiting tour group.

"Hey," Nancy called after her. "It wasn't all *my* fault!" The blond girl didn't look back. Nancy shrugged and joined her father.

"Where's Mrs. da Silva?" she asked him.

Carson shook his head. "I don't see her. She did say she'd be here."

"Yes." Nancy's eyes narrowed in thought. She was beginning to wonder about the mysterious Mrs. da Silva.

A midshipman led the tour, taking the passengers to the lower decks to see the lifeboat berths. "Luckily, we've never had to use these, but it's essential that you all know how," he instructed.

While he was demonstrating the pulley system, Nancy looked around at the passengers and crew. There were the usual groupings of elderly people, but mostly the crowd seemed like a young and very good-looking one. She wished Bess and George were there.

As she looked over her shoulder, she spotted an assistant cruise director nameplate. She raised her gaze and found that she was being studied by a pair of intense green eyes.

Oh, Bess, wouldn't you just fall over, Nancy thought. The guy was golden blond, golden tan, and, at about five feet eight inches, just Bess's size. To top it off, he had a dazzling white grin.

Just then the ship's horn sounded a deafening blast, and they began to sail out of the harbor. Nancy breathed in the fresh sea air and smiled to herself. This was going to be a great vacation!

At seven-thirty, Nancy and her father headed down to the Amethyst Deck for dinner with the captain. As they paused at the door to a small dining room, a voice behind them murmured, "You must be Nancy Drew."

Nancy whirled around and found herself staring into green eyes. "How—"

"Because I'm the ACD. It's my job to spot VIPs," the guy said with a grin. "Randy Wolfe, at your service. Will you let me show you and your father to the captain's table?"

In spite of herself, Nancy was charmed. She smiled her thanks, and the three of them crossed the dining room. Nancy gulped as she saw that the ash blond girl was seated at her table.

The blonde, Nancy soon learned, was Lynn Ashley of Savannah, Georgia. She was seated at Randy's left, and Nancy was at his right.

Randy leaned over to Nancy. "The epitome of the spoiled Southern belle," he whispered, with a slight nod in Lynn's direction. "Her aunt was taking her on this tour, but she couldn't make it at the last minute. So now it's *my* job to keep her out of the clutches of fortune hunters! What a drag!"

Nancy grinned. "Oh, I'm sure you'll find a way to have *some* fun," she replied.

She looked around at the others. Nina da Silva was seated on Carson Drew's left, still a little pale but stunning in a dark red dress that set off her beautiful emerald jewelry.

A young man named Matt Jordan sat in the

chair to Nancy's right, his wife, Melissa, next to him. The Jordans were on their honeymoon. Matt appeared to be shy. His gentle brown eyes were filled with good humor, but he'd hardly uttered a word since they sat down.

Melissa Jordan, friendly and outgoing, talked enough for both of them. Her dark eyes snapped vivaciously as she flirted a little with all the men at the table.

"Oh, Randy," Lynn Ashley gushed loudly just then, "it must be just the *most* exciting thing to be a cruise director! Why, I declare, you must have the pick of all the ladies at every dance!" She fluttered her eyelashes.

Nancy cringed inside. What a phony! she thought. I bet she's as predatory as she looks.

"Oh, it's not all a bed of roses," he said coolly to Lynn. "Sometimes I have to be polite when I don't really feel like it." Lynn nearly choked on a lettuce leaf.

Melissa Jordan broke in. "Oh, but it must be exciting to be based in exotic South America. I've read so much about Rio de Janeiro, I'm just dying to see it!" She lowered her voice and almost conspiratorially said, "They say that Rio's the place where all the big-time crooks go to spend their money and live out their lives in luxury. Do you think it's true?" she asked Captain Brant.

Brant looked pointedly at Nancy. "Why don't

you ask our resident expert on crime?" he suggested, his eyes twinkling.

Nancy winced. I wish he hadn't brought that up, she thought. But Melissa Jordan seemed not to have heard. She went on speaking. "As a matter of fact, Matt was telling me about a big emerald theft in Rio—when was it, honey?"

"About a year ago," Matt said, blushing a little.

"In fact, we heard it was never solved," Melissa continued for him. "They traced one of the crooks to a luxury cruise liner, but after that the whole thing seemed to die down. Maybe the crook is still around! I guess you should be careful of your emeralds, Mrs. da Silva."

Nancy looked at Nina da Silva and found her gaze being returned. It was an intense look, as if Mrs. da Silva were trying to tell her something. What's going on? Nancy thought. She practically kicked us out of her cabin today, but if I didn't know better, I'd say she just sent me an SOS.

Just then a lightly accented voice interrupted the conversation. "Ladies and gentlemen, allow me to introduce myself and present my compliments to the captain's special guests. I am Antonio Ribeiro, the hotel manager. It is my responsibility to ensure that your cruise is as comfortable and carefree as our hand-picked crew can make it," Ribeiro continued. "My staff and I are always at your disposal."

Tall, dark, and definitely very smooth, Nancy said to herself. She saw Ribeiro's eyes travel around the table. When they reached Nina da Silva, his smile suddenly vanished, and he gave the widow one of the nastiest stares Nancy had ever seen.

Then she saw Nina's own expression. And Nancy knew that if looks could kill, Ribeiro would drop dead then and there!

# Chapter Three

NANCY GLANCED AROUND the table. No, it hadn't been her imagination—the others had noticed the exchange, too.

After what seemed like minutes of silence, Randy leaned into Nancy. "Is it my cologne?" he asked softly, looking at her with such anxiety that she had to laugh.

That broke the tension, and soon everyone was talking again.

Still, there *was* something weird going on. Something that connected Nina da Silva with the hotel manager, Nancy knew.

But what was it?

Nancy was sure of only one thing: their meeting appeared to be a nasty surprise for them both.

"Hey, don't frown like that. Unless you really do hate my cologne, that is," said a voice in her ear. Startled, Nancy turned and found herself staring once more into the emerald green eyes of Randy Wolfe. His mouth curved in a lazy grin, and Nancy was struck by the tan that set off his even white teeth.

She smiled back. "Sorry. I'm off in my own world. But you can't fool me—you're not even wearing cologne."

The long trip from River Heights was beginning to take its toll on Nancy, and the rest of the meal passed in a haze for her.

Her father was having a great time talking with Captain Brant and Nina da Silva. Actually, Captain Brant wasn't saying much—Carson and Nina were practically ignoring him as they spoke to each other. Finally, Carson looked over at Nancy.

"You look as tired as I feel," he remarked. "I think the best thing for both of us would be to get some sleep."

"Sounds good to me," Nancy agreed. They stood up to say their good nights. Nancy noticed Carson lean down to murmur something to Nina, which made her throw back her head and laugh, her dark eyes shining.

Dad really likes her, Nancy realized. I hope it's not serious, because I'm pretty sure our attractive widow has something on her mind—and it's not romance!

The next morning, after a dreamless sleep, Nancy was up at seven. She wanted to catch Nina da Silva alone and see if she could get the woman to tell her anything more about the spiders. She can't seriously believe it was just a practical joke, can she? Nancy wondered.

When Nancy knocked at the door of Cabin O-23, it swung open. Nina da Silva was standing inside, her back to Nancy, examining a large drawing. From where Nancy stood, she could see that the drawing was a professional blueprint—it looked like the diagram of a ship much like the *Emerald Queen.*

"Good morning!" Nancy said from the doorway.

As Nina heard Nancy's voice, she whirled around, and for a split second Nancy saw alarm on her face. Then it was gone, and Nina was smiling a welcome.

"Good morning, Nancy," she said. Quickly she rolled up the blueprint and thrust it into her dresser drawer. "Did you sleep well?"

"Like a log," Nancy replied. Then she added casually, "Were those architects' plans you were looking at? Are you building something?"

"Not exactly—they're for an office complex my husband was financing when he died. I've had to take over a lot of the business he left undone. But then I'm sure you're not interested in such things."

I wonder if that's a hint to lay off, Nancy thought. Then why did I get the distinct feeling she was trying to tell me something at dinner last night?

One thing was certain—Nina had lied about the blueprint. The shape outlined on the paper was definitely that of a ship.

"I really came by to check up on you, to see if anything else had happened since you got that nasty gift yesterday. You still have no idea who might have sent it?" Nancy asked, concerned.

A frown crossed Nina's face, and she shook her head. "No, I really can't imagine who might play such a trick, but I do wish you wouldn't concern yourself." She fixed Nancy with a piercing gaze and spoke very slowly. "I assure you, it's nothing to worry about."

That implication was perfectly clear—back off! Nancy gave up.

"Well, I'm off to the pool. See you later." Nancy smiled and closed the door behind her.

"Nancy! Were you just visiting Nina?"

Carson Drew had emerged from his cabin, and Nancy kissed her father good morning as they walked along. Nancy also talked to him about what was on her mind.

"To be honest, Dad, I wasn't just visiting. I wanted to ask Mrs. da Silva some more questions about that box of spiders and about that weird exchange at dinner last night. But she wouldn't talk to me. And she lied to me about one thing—I know that for sure. I have a feeling there's something really fishy going on here, and I think that whatever it is, she may be involved."

Carson Drew frowned. "Nancy, Nina da Silva is a fine woman. Don't you see that she's the victim here? If anything, she needs our support, not our suspicion!"

Nancy sighed. This was not going to be easy. "Dad, all I'm saying is that she knows a lot that she doesn't want to tell us. And I want to know what. If someone has it in for her, wouldn't you think she'd want to tell someone? Wouldn't she want help?"

"She has a right to her privacy, Nancy!" Carson Drew was getting angry now. "I respect that right. And I'm surprised that you don't seem to. Give it a rest!"

Nancy stared at her father, hurt. He grimaced and rubbed the back of his neck. "I'm sorry. That sounded harsh. I guess I'm on edge."

After a short silence Nancy said, "Sorry, Dad. I'm going for a swim now. See you at lunch."

They parted tensely. As Nancy stepped up from the stairway onto the Pearl Deck, where the pool was, she felt a lump rise in her throat. Was she really out of line? Would her work always drive away the people she loved?

The sun streamed out of a cloudless sky, and the sea breeze caressed Nancy's cheeks as she strolled aft along the deck. She leaned over the railing and gazed at the frothing wake the ship tossed out to the side.

In spite of herself, she began to feel cheerful again—it was impossible not to on such a gorgeous day. The only thing missing right then was Ned Nickerson by her side. Nancy closed her eyes. She could almost see and hear him.

Immediately her eyes flew open again. She *did* hear a man's voice, but it was definitely not Ned's. Somebody was speaking in a harsh whisper—Nancy strained to make out the words, but the voice was coming from around the curve of the stern, or rear, railing.

A woman's voice broke in, angry but tinged with fear. "What do you want from me?"

It was Nina da Silva! Nancy was positive of that. She edged quietly along the railing, moving closer to the two people.

The man spoke again, louder this time. Nancy listened intently, her eyes narrowed in concentration. The harsh voice had a core of coldness to it that chilled her for a second, even in the warm sunlight.

"Don't play games with me, Nina. You know I want the map. I know all about your double-crossing husband—and I have proof—so you'd be well advised simply to hand the map over and keep your mouth shut!"

"You're a fool if you think you can frighten me. I've learned some things—"

*"Aaa-chooo!"*

Disaster! A brisk breeze had blown Nancy's reddish blond hair forward across her face. The silky strands had tickled her nose, and before she knew it, she had sneezed.

The woman's voice stopped abruptly. There was a sound of rapid footsteps moving toward Nancy. What now? I can't bluff this one out in front of Mrs. da Silva, she realized. I've got to disappear!

A row of cabins faced the railing on this deck. Although she knew it would be locked, Nancy tried the first door she came to.

To her surprise, it opened.

Nancy peered inside. The shades were down, and the darkened cabin seemed to be empty. She ducked inside and shut the door carefully, wincing at the almost soundless click of the latch.

Nancy stood perfectly still, straining to catch any noise that might tell her where her unknown pursuer was. She knew she wouldn't like to be alone in a room with him.

Footsteps came right up to the door—and then stopped. Nancy strode back a foot, ready to launch a kick at whoever was outside the door.

Her right foot landed on something that gave a little. Someone swore quietly in the darkness and a strong hand was clamped across Nancy's mouth. Her arms were pinned with another arm.

Nancy *definitely* wasn't alone.

# Chapter Four

NANCY COULD DO nothing. If she put up a fight, she'd attract whoever was outside the cabin. And she knew that that would be a mistake.

After the footsteps outside retreated down the deck, Nancy drove her elbow into the ribs of the person holding her. There was a muffled groan, and then she was released.

Nancy reached over and flicked on the light switch. As brightness flooded the cabin, a male voice said, "Some greeting! I guess it would be dumb to hope you were following me."

It was Randy Wolfe! Nancy stared at him in astonishment. "What are you doing here?" she exclaimed.

Randy dropped his gaze. He seemed a little embarrassed. "I, uh, came in here to get something for Lynn Ashley—it's her cabin," he said.

"In the dark?" Nancy asked.

"Actually, I was just leaving when you came charging in. Then when you backed into me, I lost my balance—that was why I grabbed you. Which was kind of fun, until you used that kung fu elbow on me." He grinned at her and massaged his ribs. "Now *you* tell *me*—I was pretty surprised when the door opened and you dashed in. Something wrong?"

"No. I—I was just looking for the linen room. I forgot my towel, and I thought there might be a storeroom on this deck, so I wouldn't have to go all the way back to my cabin," Nancy said, improvising. Boy, Drew, that's one of your flimsier covers, she reproved herself.

Randy didn't question it, though. He seemed preoccupied. "Yeah, well, I'd better get back to the pool before Lynn throws one of her Southern belle tantrums," he mumbled. He seemed embarrassed—Nancy wondered if it was because she had discovered him fetching and carrying for Lynn.

She cast a curious eye around the room. "So this is Lynn's cabin, huh?" she said. A tangle of jewelry lay as if carelessly tossed on a table by the door. Something about the jewelry caught Nancy's eye, and she picked up a strand of seed pearls to peer more closely at it.

Suddenly she chuckled. Each of the pearls was marred by a faint seam. They were fake! So the glamorous Lynn Ashley wasn't as rich as she wanted everyone to think!

"What's so funny?" Randy demanded.

"Nothing," she answered, still smiling. "Come on—I just realized I have my towel right here in my bag. I'll walk with you."

As they walked, Randy took Nancy's arm just above the elbow. "Have you ever danced on deck in the moonlight?" he asked. A dimple deepened in his cheek as he smiled.

Nancy laughed. "Is that one of your duties?" she parried. "Tough life!"

They reached the pool. It was crowded already, but Lynn was nowhere in sight. Randy leaned against the diving board. "Have you?" he persisted.

"No, I haven't. But you wouldn't neglect your duty, would you? I'm sure all your dances are already promised to Lynn," Nancy reminded him, grinning.

"I'll make sure to save a couple of slow ones for you," Randy said softly and reached out to smooth Nancy's hair from her face. His fingers trailed lightly over her bare shoulder, making her skin tingle. Nancy thought it was about time to change the subject.

"So—uh—how long have you been assigned to the *Emerald Queen?"* She moved away casually.

"Oh, I'm new. This is only my second cruise on the *Emerald,*" Randy said. "I started out working on another South American ship with the Sea Queen line, but about a year ago the company transferred me to their European branch. They needed an all-American type who could also speak Portuguese. My family lived in Rio for a while when I was a kid, so I was perfect for the job.

"I spent last year on the Portugal-to-Morocco route. But I like this side of the world better, so I asked to be transferred back." He spread his hands. "And here I am, meeting you. I'm telling you, fate has decreed that we get together!"

Nancy decided to ignore that one. "Do you like the people you work with?" she asked. Casually, she added, "That guy Ribeiro, the hotel manager —he seems a little unfriendly."

Randy frowned. "Antonio? I don't know him very well. He keeps to himself. But he's pleasant enough."

"I could have sworn he and Mrs. da Silva recognized each other at dinner last night," Nancy went on. "Why do you think they didn't say hello or anything?"

Randy only shrugged, but his frown deepened. I bet he knows something, Nancy thought. And I want to know what it is!

She plopped herself down in a poolside lounge chair and took off her cotton cover-up. Shading her eyes with her hand, she looked up at Randy and grinned.

He drew up another lounge and sat down, looking thoughtfully at the water.

"Don't look so serious!" she chided. "I'm just naturally curious. I love to come up with stories about people. Now—Ribeiro. Do you think he has a shady past? I'd definitely be inclined to cast him as a villain, wouldn't you?"

Randy relaxed. "Well, I'll tell you one thing—" he began, when a silky female voice cut in.

"My goodness, you two are serious." Nancy turned and saw Lynn Ashley standing behind her. Lynn seemed to have materialized out of thin air. How much had she overheard?

Lynn's light blond hair was artistically tousled, and she wore a white string bikini that accented her perfect salon tan. Nancy had to admit that she was attractive—in a brittle way.

Lynn gave Nancy a sugary smile. "Mind if I cut in?" She moved close to Randy. "You did promise to teach me how to play shuffleboard, remember?" she drawled.

She took Randy's arm and towed him away. He mouthed "Help" to Nancy over his shoulder, and she laughed out loud.

"You're on your own," she whispered. Randy rolled his eyes in mock horror.

Rats! Lynn sure had great timing. Or was

there more to her interrupting than I thought? Nancy suddenly wondered. Maybe Lynn really was listening in. And maybe she was trying to warn Randy to stop talking!

This was getting her nowhere. She was beginning to suspect everyone on the ship of being involved in a gigantic conspiracy. And she didn't even know what they could possibly be hiding.

Nancy met her father for lunch on the outdoor terrace of the Opal Lounge. He'd spent most of the morning with Nina da Silva.

"Nina's quite a woman," he commented. "She was born in the States, but she went to Brazil to teach," Carson Drew continued. "She met and married Hector da Silva about five years later, but she went on teaching and working with the local poor people until his death last year. She didn't need to teach for a living—he was a wealthy shipping magnate—but she wanted to."

"A shipping magnate?" Nancy was interested. If Nina da Silva had shipping interests, that would explain the blueprint in her cabin—but not why she had lied about it.

Carson nodded. "She's had to take over Hector's various enterprises since his death, I gather, which is why she's given up teaching. But she plans to resume as soon as she can. That's dedication, wouldn't you say?"

"It sure is." Nancy decided to tell him about

the conversation she'd overheard. "Dad, this morning—" she began.

"Yes, this morning," her father broke in. He leaned forward. "Listen, Nan, I'm sorry if I sounded harsh this morning. You know I love you very much, and I also respect what you do. I believe you've helped a lot of people—"

"Uh-oh, I think I hear a 'but' coming," Nancy said.

"But even if Nina's having some sort of trouble, it would be wrong to intrude if she hasn't asked for help. We have no evidence of any kind of criminal activity."

"What if I find some?" Nancy asked.

Carson Drew sighed. "That's what's at issue here. Do you have the right to go digging into someone else's life, just on a shadowy suspicion? A *suspicion* of a suspicion? I don't think so. And unless she invites our help, I have to respect her privacy. I hope you'll do the same," Carson said earnestly.

Nancy squirmed in her seat, not answering her father. How could she promise to go against all her instincts?

Glancing up, she saw a couple walk past with badminton racquets in their hands. She remembered then that she'd promised the Jordans she'd play a few games with them! Glad to be off the hook, she stood up.

"Dad," she said, holding out her hand to her

father. "Matt and Melissa Jordan have challenged the Drew dynasty to a badminton tournament. Let's go show them what we're made of."

Carson Drew looked apologetic. "Actually, Nina and I are going to meet in the solarium and soak up some sun."

"Oh. Uh, sounds great." Nancy hid her disappointment, but as she was walking back to her cabin to change, she couldn't help feeling a little hurt.

It was only the second day of the cruise, and already her father had made plans that didn't include her! What had happened to their family vacation? With the appearance of Nina da Silva, it had gone down the drain in more ways than one.

"Oh, Nancy, there's Randy Wolfe. Isn't he *gorgeous!*" At Nancy's raised eyebrows, Melissa Jordan blushed a little and giggled. "It's a good thing Matt's not listening, but I'm just expressing an opinion! I'm allowed—I'm an old married lady."

Nancy had to laugh. Melissa couldn't be much older than she was.

They were at the captain's reception now, in one of the large ultraplush cocktail lounges that dotted the ship. This was where the officers and passengers were supposed to get acquainted, and Nancy was hoping she'd see Antonio Ribeiro.

She definitely wanted to talk to him, although she hadn't yet decided what to say.

She didn't have to look far—Ribeiro suddenly appeared out of the crowd in front of them, smiling and nodding his head once. Nancy blinked. He was wearing a heavy, musky cologne that clung to him like a cloak. "Ah, the captain's guests!" he said, his voice smooth as silk. "I trust you are enjoying the cruise so far?"

"Oh, it's *wonderful,*" Nancy gushed and jumped in before Melissa could say anything. Here was her chance. "We're having a fantastic time!

"The ship is just so huge," she went on, improvising rapidly. "I don't know how you manage to find your way around. You must need a *map!*"

Ribeiro smiled indulgently. "I've learned to do without."

"Well, I definitely need one." With what she hoped was an airhead giggle, Nancy brought out her next line. "Mrs. da Silva says she has a map she'll lend me. Isn't that nice of her?"

Ribeiro's eyes narrowed. He gave Nancy a long look. "Very nice indeed," he said at last. Then he excused himself and moved on to a cluster of older women.

She'd definitely gotten his attention! She was sure now that it *had* been his voice that morning, threatening Mrs. da Silva. But it was impossible for her to tell whether or not he was suspicious of *her*.

Melissa nudged her. "Did I miss something?"

Nancy shook her head. "I'm not sure what happened myself."

Nancy fumbled through her bag for the key to her cabin. That night was the second-night formal dinner, and she didn't have much time to get ready after the captain's reception.

She turned the key in the lock and, as the door swung open, was greeted by a sweet, heady scent. Someone had sent her a huge arrangement of gardenias!

She smiled; they must be from her father. "Thanks, Dad," she said, picking up the bouquet from the dressing table. As her eye fell on the florist's card lying beside the flowers, the cloying scent of the gardenias suddenly threatened to choke her.

The message was simple:

To Nancy Drew.
For Your Funeral.

# Chapter Five

NANCY BLANCHED. SHE crumpled the card, tossed it aside, and resolved to find and stop whoever had sent it.

As she changed into a peach-colored dress with a flared skirt and matching high-heeled pumps, Nancy started feeling a little better—and a lot more angry.

First, the spiders in Nina's cabin, and now this. Nancy picked up the crumpled note, smoothed it out, and tucked it in her dresser drawer. It was time to get down to business.

Seated at the captain's table, Nancy studied the other diners. Occupied with her own thoughts, she was unable to be social.

Lynn Ashley was overdressed in a low-cut silvery dress. She was wearing the fake seed pearls around her neck, Nancy noticed, and hid a grin.

As usual, Lynn was alternately flirting with Randy and sulking when he didn't respond.

"Well, Randy Wolfe!" Nancy overheard her saying. "That's just the most exciting story I've ever heard! Do tell me about Rio. Is it as dangerous as they say? Would a young girl on her own need an escort?"

"Oh, I'm sure you'll find plenty of guys anxious to escort you," Randy replied. Obviously, he had taken an instant dislike to Lynn.

Nancy had to admit, maybe he had a good reason. Lynn Ashley appeared to be selfish, spoiled, and ruthless when it came to guys. Now she was looking past Randy to bat her eyelashes at Matt Jordan, who looked embarrassed.

Was Lynn as ruthless about other things? Nancy wondered. Was she involved in the mystery surrounding Nina da Silva? They didn't seem to know each other, but maybe . . .

Now—Antonio Ribeiro. As the hotel manager, he could have secretly arranged for the flowers and card to be delivered to Nancy. And it was quite clear there were hostile feelings between him and Nina. Yes, as a villain, he was almost too perfect.

What about Nina herself? She seemed to be a victim, but was she hiding something? Nancy still wondered why she wouldn't guess who might have put the box of spiders in her room. Was she trying to protect someone? But who and why?

Nancy studied her father, chatting with Nina da Silva. He looks so happy, she thought with a pang. I hope he doesn't get hurt. If only he'd listen to my warnings, but so far he hasn't been responsive.

"Hey, blue eyes, can I at least have a dance after dinner?" Randy said softly. "I don't want to seem conceited, but I've got to be better-looking than that lobster on your plate!"

Nancy looked up and smiled at him. "Just a few things on my mind, I guess."

"A couple of fast dances will clear out those cobwebs in no time!" Randy said with a wink.

Cobwebs! Nancy's toes curled as she remembered the spiders in the chocolate box. Could Randy have said that on purpose? Were those green eyes as friendly as they looked?

Out loud, she laughed. "Okay, you win. One dance, and then I want to study the stars for a while."

What she really wanted was a chance to take a look at Ribeiro's cabin. Maybe something there would answer a few of her questions.

Nancy felt increasingly tense as dinner came to an end and the party moved on to the dance floor. Standing beside the band with Randy and the Jordans, Nancy felt more than a little jealous as she watched Melissa and Matt. They were so much in love, and she really missed Ned!

"What a wonderful night!" Melissa said. "This trip is everything I thought it would be, and more."

Nancy nodded. *More* was definitely the right word for it! Suddenly she had an idea. If she could get Melissa to cover for her, she just might sneak the time she needed to search Ribeiro's room.

"Melissa, I've got something in my eye," said Nancy quickly. "Do you think you could come to the lounge with me and take a look? I hate to drag you away from the dancing, but it hurts."

"Sure," said Melissa, and the two weaved their way through the crowd toward the ladies' lounge.

Once inside, Nancy turned to Melissa and heaved a sigh of relief. "Thanks for the exit cue," she said, joking. "Much as I like Randy Wolfe, he was holding onto me just a little too tightly. He's a nice guy, but I'm starting to think he's taking his job a bit too seriously."

Melissa laughed. "But, Nancy," she said, "I think it would be fun to get all his attention. The other girls are dying for a chance at him!"

Delicately changing the subject, Nancy said, "I know this may be asking a lot, but I have to get away by myself for a few minutes. Do you think you could cover for me?"

Melissa's eyes widened. "But, Nancy, what would I tell them?"

Nancy thought fast. She didn't want to make Melissa nervous or suspicious. "Melissa, it's important to me. Randy doesn't know I have a boyfriend. I've just got to have a little time to think things over before it goes too far—and someone gets hurt."

"All right, Nancy," said Melissa doubtfully, "but what do I tell them? How long will you be gone? I can't say you fell overboard!"

"Tell them I broke the heel off my shoe. Tell them I ran my stocking. Come on, Melissa, a million things like that happen every day! You can do it. Just make something up."

Melissa nodded. "I do sympathize, I really do. Don't worry, I'll think of something. Now, get going or they'll think we *both* fell overboard!"

Nancy opened the door and, after a quick glance around, stole out on deck. Once she was around the bend, she took off her heels and ran down to the Amethyst Deck, where the officers had their cabins. She scanned the nameplates outside the cabin doors. Carruthers, Baldwin—Ribeiro! Luckily his cabin was the third one she came to.

Nancy dug in her evening bag and pulled out her nail file. It wasn't the ideal tool, but it had a little cuticle pusher that should work.

Careful not to make a noise, she inserted the file into the lock and jiggled it gently until the knob turned under her hand. After a quick glance around her, Nancy slipped inside the darkened cabin and relocked the door.

The room reeked of Ribeiro's heavy, musky cologne. The scent filled Nancy's lungs and made her want to cough.

Nancy flashed her tiny penlight around the room until she spotted a desk against the wall. She went carefully through each drawer, but all she found were ship's receipts for food, wine, and other supplies.

Finally, in the back of the bottom drawer, she found something that looked promising—a plain white envelope, stuffed full. She opened it. It was some kind of financial statement with a wrinkled letter, addressed to *R,* attached. Holding the light closer, Nancy tried to decipher the crabbed handwriting.

Then she realized why she couldn't read it. It was all in Portuguese! Of course. Ribeiro was Brazilian—he spoke Portuguese. Nancy was fluent in Spanish and French but not this!

Looking again at the letter, she picked out one familiar word. *Mapa.* She guessed that meant "map."

Then two names caught her eye: *Nina* in the second paragraph, all in capitals, and the letter was signed *da Silva.*

Aha, Nancy thought. At last I've got something

in writing. And it links Nina da Silva with Mr. Smooth Ribeiro!

Suddenly, there was a noise at the door, and a key scraped in the lock.

Ribeiro!

Her heart pounding, Nancy looked for an escape route. Nothing! She shoved the papers back in the drawer and dashed for the closet.

The cabin door opened, and Nancy held her breath as footsteps moved heavily over to the desk and stopped. A drawer was opened, carefully, and papers rustled. Then more steps, heading right for the closet!

Now you've done it, thought Nancy. Cornered in a closet, of all places.

She tried not to sneeze or cough from the overpowering smell of cologne and pushed herself farther back into the hanging suit jackets.

The door was yanked open then. A black-sleeved arm reached in—straight for Nancy's throat!

# Chapter Six

NANCY SLOWLY SLID down against the closet wall, praying she could stay out of the reach of the groping hands.

One hand pushed several coats aside and came to rest on an evening jacket. Nancy almost fainted as Ribeiro took the jacket out and closed the door with a sharp click.

She listened as he changed and left the cabin. Cautiously, she nudged the door open and slid out. She stepped quickly to the desk and opened the bottom drawer.

The papers were gone!

Nancy clenched her teeth, furious with herself. The perfect chance to prove to her father that there *was* a mystery involving Nina da Silva and Antonio Ribeiro, and she had acted like an inexperienced amateur, losing her only piece of hard evidence and almost getting herself caught.

Discouraged, Nancy made her way back to the dance, where Randy spotted her immediately and sauntered over.

"Hey, blue eyes," he greeted her, "that was some disappearing act. Let's dance. I'm not missing my chance again, that's for sure!"

Actually, Nancy would have loved to dance—to a fast song, that is. She needed to work out some of her tension. But Randy pulled her out to the middle of the floor, just as a slow, romantic song was beginning.

"Now, this isn't bad, is it?" he whispered in her ear. One of his hands strayed up her back, and he began playing with a lock of her hair.

Nancy pulled back and looked into the handsome emerald green eyes and took a deep ragged breath. It was time to get a few things straight.

"Look, this might not be the best time, but I think you should know my boyfriend is meeting the cruise in Rio," she said, trying to keep a little distance between them as they danced.

"So, we still have two whole days together," replied Randy cheerfully. "After all, I'm only doing my job, making sure the passengers are entertained."

Finally, the dance over, Nancy and Randy rejoined the Jordans. Apparently deciding that Nancy could take care of herself, Melissa shot her a covert look, grasped Matt's hand, and stood up.

"I think it's bedtime for us," she said, yawning. "We've got a big day tomorrow. See you all at breakfast."

Matt added his good-nights, and the newlyweds headed for the Pearl Deck.

"I'd better go, too," Nancy told Randy. "It's been a long day." Randy walked her to the elevators.

"Good night, blue eyes," he said. "Sleep well." After giving her a light kiss on the cheek, he strode back toward the thinning group of dancers.

Nancy felt exhausted when she got to her cabin. She tried to sort through the events of the day, from the threats she had overheard to the letter in Ribeiro's desk. Somehow, she had a feeling that that letter was crucial to the case. If only she knew what the case was.

Finally, Nancy drifted into an uneasy sleep.

The next morning at breakfast Randy made an announcement: "Today is our first stop. We'll be taking groups ashore to Paranagua. After a tour of the town, there'll be time for shopping and sightseeing. Launches leave in an hour."

He sauntered over to the table where Nancy sat

with her father and the Jordans. "Too bad I can't come along," he said. "Unfortunately, this job isn't all fun and games. We get more than enough paperwork to earn our keep."

Nancy smiled sympathetically. "Well, we'll just have to get along without you, I guess." Actually, she was relieved at the prospect of spending some time with her father—if she could get him alone.

She walked with Carson Drew as he headed to his cabin. "Mind if I tag along, Dad? There are a few things I'd like to fill you in on."

Carson frowned. "Nancy, are you still under the impression that Nina da Silva is in trouble? I assure you—"

"But, Dad, just listen to me for a moment! Yesterday I heard someone threatening her, and I'm ninety-nine percent sure—"

Carson cut her off. "Nancy, ninety-nine percent isn't good enough. You'd better be absolutely positive if you're going to ask any personal questions. Nina came on this cruise for a vacation, just like the rest of us, and I know she values her privacy."

Nancy was astonished—and hurt. Her father was usually willing to listen. She couldn't remember the last time he'd treated her this way. Was it because he was getting too involved with Nina da Silva? She gritted her teeth, determined to make her point.

"I have evidence, Dad. At least, I had it—a letter—but I lost it before I could get a copy. Believe me, Dad, I don't want to make waves, but I honestly think there's something going on—and I know they're trying to keep me from finding out what it is."

"How do you know that?" her father asked skeptically.

"Dad, last evening I got a bouquet of gardenias. The card that came with them said they were for my funeral, but it wasn't signed. I think that's a clear threat, don't you? And I got them right after I started asking questions about those spiders in Mrs. da Silva's room. Please don't try to tell me these things are just sick jokes."

"Nancy, why didn't you tell me about this before?" Carson's concern overcame his annoyance.

Nancy shrugged. "You would have told me to leave the case alone."

"You're right. I *would* have—for your own safety. But I still don't see how any of this connects Nina with any crime. I've changed my mind—I think we've got to go over and ask her if she needs our help."

Together Nancy and her father walked the short distance to Nina da Silva's cabin. At their knock, she opened the door and stared at them, surprised. Then she stepped back to let them in.

Carson seemed uncomfortable. "Nina," he

began, "Nancy and I were wondering if you'd like to join us on the shore trip."

"Thank you, but I've some letters to write here," said Nina.

Nancy took the plunge. "Mrs. da Silva, we don't want to intrude, but after that box you received I felt a little alarmed. Then I thought I heard someone talking to you by the pool—he sounded as if he were threatening you. I didn't intend to eavesdrop, but I *would* like to help if you're having trouble.

"Is there anything you have that someone might want badly enough to threaten you?"

Nina glanced at Carson, then turned to Nancy with a polite smile. "Of course not. I have no idea who might play such a *joke* on me. And I assure you that there's no trouble of any kind."

"Nancy," Carson said in an embarrassed tone, "let's leave Nina to write her letters. Nina, I do apologize—sometimes my daughter's professional zeal gets the better of her."

Nancy couldn't believe it! She'd never heard her father talk about her this way before. Her face burning with humiliation, she turned to go.

Nina seemed lost in thought, but then she took a deep breath. "Carson, there *is* a small matter I'd like to discuss with you and Nancy, but I need to think it over. Perhaps this evening when you return? Now, I mustn't keep you from Paranagua."

Nancy and Carson turned to go. Nancy looked back at the elegantly dressed woman. "Mrs. da Silva, I'm sorry if we disturbed you."

Nina nodded, and Nancy and Carson headed out to the Main Deck where the launches were loading for the shore trip.

Nancy felt uncomfortable with her father. She knew he hadn't meant to hurt her, but his words had cut very deeply.

Since they had a few minutes before the last boat left, Nancy decided to run over to the flower shop to see if she could find out who had sent the gardenias. She knew the sender had probably covered his tracks thoroughly, but at least it would give her time to collect her thoughts before she talked to her father again.

The ship's florist, a kindly-looking man in his fifties, seemed surprised at Nancy's questions.

"Someone left a note for the order," he said. "It's not uncommon. It was left with a sealed envelope—we keep a basket of cards and envelopes on the counter so that people can write private messages if they like. I simply assumed they were from your father since they were charged to his cabin. I hope there was no problem?"

"No," replied Nancy cheerfully, "but I loved the arrangement, and I just wanted to find out if you still had the order so I could have another made up exactly like it."

"Well, miss, I'm sorry," said the florist. "We

don't usually keep orders once they've been delivered."

Nancy gave up and, after thanking him, just had time to catch the last boat with Carson Drew.

Paranagua *was* beautiful. At last Carson Drew and Nancy had a whole day to wander around, enjoying the sights. Most of the other passengers —Lynn Ashley in the lead—headed straight for the shops after the tour, but the Drews decided to explore the town instead.

But Nancy was having a hard time enjoying herself. In the sunny weather the whitewashed shops and houses gleamed, and waves of heat rippled off them so that they seemed to float in their gardens of exotic flowers. Nancy knew she had to break the tension somehow.

"Dad," she said tentatively. "I'm sorry if I embarrassed you in front of Mrs. da Silva."

Carson Drew looked at his daughter. "Well," he said slowly, "maybe I did overreact—a little. It's just that I wanted to relax and enjoy this vacation, but it seems that you're determined to go around suspecting people of all sorts of things."

Nancy knew he had a point. "I know there's not much to go on," she admitted, "but I also know there's something Mrs. da Silva wants to hide from us. It could be dangerous for her."

"Let's forget it for now, at least," said Carson,

reaching over to squeeze his daughter's hand. Nancy could feel the tension ebbing a little as she squeezed back.

Together, father and daughter explored the historic town. Nancy was secretly glad that Nina da Silva had remained on board. At last she was spending time with her father—alone.

At around four o'clock, they found a tiny café off the picturesque main square. They sat there sipping iced tea, watching the town pass by in the peaceful afternoon sun.

"This is the life, Dad," said Nancy, as they reluctantly stood up and stretched, ready to leave the café to head back to the dock. "I think I could have stayed here forever."

Carson laughed. "You'd go crazy without Ned and your friends, and you know it," he replied affectionately. "Besides, River Heights wouldn't be the same without its famous detective."

"Hey, Nancy!" a voice called. Looking up, Nancy saw Randy Wolfe waving to her from across the street. As she was walking over to meet him, she heard a roar as an engine was kicked to life. She turned.

A silver motorcycle was pulling out of a side street. The sun reflecting off it, the chrome fittings, and the driver's full mirrored helmet blinded her for a moment.

She blinked once to clear her eyes. And when she opened them again, she saw the cycle heading straight for her—at about fifty miles an hour!

# Chapter Seven

IT HAPPENED SO quickly Nancy had no time to react. One second the bike was thundering toward her—and the next she was flying through the air. A pair of tanned arms had wrapped around her in a flying tackle.

She rolled in a jumble of arms and legs to the safety of the high wooden curb as the motorcycle's tires sped by, inches from her face. The growl of the cycle's engine sank in pitch and then faded into the distance.

"We've got to stop meeting like this," came Randy Wolfe's breathless voice right in Nancy's ear. Pale and dusty but grinning, he disengaged himself and got to his feet.

"Wha—" Nancy sat up dazedly. She spat out some dust and rubbed her eyes. "What are *you* doing here?"

"Nancy! Are you all right?" Nancy's father came running to her. He knelt down, his face taut with anxiety. "I'll call an ambulance!"

Nancy put a hand to her forehead. "I think I'm okay," she said. "Please, don't bother with an ambulance. I'll be fine." She held out a hand to her father, and he pulled her up.

Carson Drew turned to Randy. "That was one of the most incredible rescues I've ever seen. I don't know how to thank you."

"Nor I," Nancy said. "You saved my life."

Randy looked embarrassed. "Just part of my job," he said lightly. Then, more soberly, he added, "It's a good thing I just happened to be coming out of that shop over there. You've got to watch out for drivers in these small towns. They don't know what traffic laws are."

Nancy was silent. She wasn't at all sure that the driver of the motorcycle was a local, or that her "accident" had been unintended.

"I came over with the return launches to pick up a sweater for my kid sister," Randy explained. "I think we'd better head to the docks now."

They were joined just then by the Jordans and Lynn Ashley. Nancy was surprised to learn that Lynn had gone off by herself for most of the day.

"What was she doing all day?" Nancy whispered to Melissa as they hurried to the launches.

"Probably figuring out how to cheat the local craftsmen out of their wares," Melissa whispered back. "You know, Nancy, I hate to be catty, but that girl was just born mean—except when it comes to men."

Nancy looked at Lynn, who was clinging to Randy and laughing at something he had said. Mean enough to hurt someone? she wondered. Mean enough to try to kill me?

Back on the *Emerald Queen,* Nancy was on deck, heading to her cabin, when she felt a hand on her arm. It was Randy, without a spark of humor in his dazzling green eyes now.

"We need to talk," he said quietly. "I think we both know that that was no accident back there in Paranagua. I saw the way that cyclist headed straight for you. And I know you noticed it, too. I'm not prying, but it seems to me that you've made an enemy. And for some reason, I don't want you to get hurt, blue eyes."

Nancy felt a rush of gratitude. "I've got to clean up and change, but meet me in the Opal Lounge in fifteen minutes," she said, grinning. "Have I got a story for you!"

Twenty minutes later, over frosty tropical fruit shakes, Nancy was outlining the case for Randy. At last, when she had finished, Randy let out a long whistle. "So, what do we do next?"

Nancy was grateful for the "we." "For now, nothing," she said. "I need to get some answers from Nina da Silva before we do anything. But my dad insists I let her come to me."

Randy nodded. "Sounds good, chief." He looked at his watch and stood up. "I've got to go run the bingo game for the senior citizens' group. Then I have to stand on a ladder and drape streamers for the Emerald Ball tonight. Such is the glamorous life of an ACD."

Nancy walked out with him, and he gave her a quick kiss on the cheek. "Watch out for tall, dark strangers," he cautioned. Then he was gone.

Nancy climbed the companionway, or stairs, to the Pearl Deck, hoping to find Melissa and Matt. She ran into Captain Brant first. He was leaning on a rail, watching a shuffleboard game.

"I never knew shuffleboard was a combat skill!" Nancy said, joining him.

"It's like pool. Some players take it pretty seriously." Captain Brant chuckled. "Why, Nina da Silva's husband, Hector, was the worst loser I ever met! He used to sulk for days whenever anyone beat him. Which, thank goodness, was rare."

"How well do you know Mrs. da Silva?" Nancy asked in a casual voice.

"Oh, Nina and I go way back. I knew her brother in the States. When I came down to Brazil with the Merchant Marine, I always stayed with her and Hector. Even took a cruise on the *Emerald Queen* with them. Hector used to own this cruise line, did you know?"

"No, I didn't know." Nancy's heart suddenly beat faster. Another piece in the puzzle! But where did it go?

"That's right. He ran into some money trouble a couple of years ago and had to sell the line to a big corporation. But he stayed on as general manager of this ship. That's when I came aboard. He was a good-hearted man, Hector was. A little impulsive, maybe, but good-hearted to a fault."

"What exactly does a general manager do?" Nancy hardly heard the last part of Captain Brant's speech. Her mind was racing. She had the feeling that she'd just stumbled on an important fact.

"He's the company liaison. Travels on all the cruises, oversees the ship's management—he's the final authority on everything outside the actual, mechanical running of the ship. I don't hold with it on general principle, but I'd trust Hector not to interfere with a captain's command of his ship."

Nancy nodded absently. So Hector da Silva had traveled with the *Emerald Queen!* There was the link she was looking for between the da Silvas and Antonio Ribeiro. If, that is, Ribeiro had been on the ship for at least a year, since before Hector da Silva had died.

Clearly, she needed to get more information on da Silva and the cruise line, but where? Suddenly an idea struck.

Excusing herself, she hurried down to the radio room, where a bored-looking woman officer sat at a lighted panel, reading a romance novel.

"Hi. I need to make a ship-to-shore call to the United States," Nancy said.

The woman looked up. "It's all yours." She yawned, waving at the console and headset. Then her eyes strayed back to her novel.

Nancy waited, but the woman just sat there. "Um—it's a personal call," Nancy said apologetically.

The radio officer's face fell. With a single doleful sniff, she climbed to her feet and left the room. Nancy quickly dialed the number of the River Heights *Morning Record,* hoping to catch her friend, reporter Ann Granger, in the paper's office.

"Ann, it's Nancy Drew," she said when she heard Ann's voice on the other end. "Listen, I don't have a lot of time to talk. I need some information. Can you help?"

"No problem, Nancy," Ann said. "Sounds like your vacation got a little boring. What's the case?"

"I wish I knew." Nancy sighed. "I'll give you the whole story when I get back." Nancy told Ann what she needed. "I'll call you tomorrow from Rio, and see what you've got for me. Bye."

She hung up and walked outside. The radio officer was sitting in a deck chair, scanning her book without much interest.

"Thanks," Nancy called. "It was *wonderful* talking to him."

Now for Nina da Silva. She said she'd talk to Dad and me tonight, Nancy thought. It's evening now. *And* I've got a tangible lead—the link between Hector da Silva and Ribeiro qualifies, doesn't it? Dad'll understand.

Nancy decided to take the elevator up the three levels to the Opal Deck. There was a group of kids about her own age waiting for the elevator, and she exchanged a few words with one of the girls, who seemed very friendly.

Boy, this ship really is huge, she thought as she watched them get off the elevator at the Sapphire Deck. I've never even seen any of them before!

She walked along the rail to Cabin O-23 and knocked on the door. No answer. She knocked again, a little louder. The door swung open under her rapping knuckles.

"Mrs. da Silva?" Nancy called. There was no reply, so she stepped inside, flicking on the light as she did so. She felt a sudden chill.

The cabin was empty—much too empty. It was cleaned out as if no one had ever been there. All of Mrs. da Silva's personal items were gone from the dressing table and the nightstand. The bed had been stripped, and new linens lay folded at its foot. The closet door stood open, and Nancy could see there was nothing inside.

Nancy crossed to the dressing table and yanked open the drawers. Not a sign of the mysterious blueprint. Could that have been the "map" Ribeiro wanted? No—he could have obtained his own plan of the ship easily enough.

There was nothing here. Nancy moved toward the door. Then, frowning, she turned back for one last look. Her eyes narrowed thoughtfully. Where could Nina have gone?

Suddenly the room went black as the door behind her banged shut. Nancy headed swiftly for the bedside light, but an arm caught her from behind, squeezing her ribs painfully.

There was a metallic click, and Nancy's heart leapt. She knew what that sound meant.

A switchblade.

# Chapter Eight

AS SHE FELT her attacker raise the blade to her throat, Nancy went limp.

Surprised, the attacker shifted his grasp, which was what Nancy had hoped he'd do. It gave her the second she needed to seize his knife hand in both of hers and squeeze—hard. The man gasped, and the knife dropped noiselessly to the thick carpet.

They both dove for it at once. Nancy could hear her attacker grunting as he struggled to keep a hold on her. His groping fingers must have found the blade, for she soon felt the chill of steel against her throat.

Nancy reached behind her and started to rake his face with her nails, but he dropped the knife and caught her hand. Snarling, he twisted her arm painfully behind her back, hauling her to her feet.

Nancy kicked back with her right leg, and they went sprawling to the floor again.

For a moment they were face to face, so close that Nancy could smell the clean scent of soap that clung to him. He was wearing a diving mask, and because the curtains were drawn across the porthole Nancy couldn't make out his features. But she knew instinctively he was deadly.

*"AAAAAGGHH!"* Nancy screamed at the top of her lungs—right in the man's face. It was a tactic she had learned in a martial arts class, and it worked well. The man flinched as if the sound were something solid.

Nancy didn't stay to finish the fight. Scrambling to her feet, she ran to the door and yanked it open. "Help!" she yelled into the deserted corridor as she darted through the doorway.

She raced to the end of the hall and half ran, half fell down the metal steps of the companionway.

Nancy was going so fast that she couldn't stop herself when she saw a crewman hurrying up the steps directly in her path. She caromed into him, and they both tumbled down the steps, landing in a heap at the bottom. Nancy was on her feet immediately.

"Sorry," she panted. "Please, come with me quickly! Mrs. da Silva is missing, and Antonio Ribeiro just tried to kill me!"

"Senorita?" the young crewman yelped, looking at her as if she had just stepped out of a spaceship. He scrambled to his feet and straightened his steward's tunic. "Mr. Ribeiro is trying to *kill* you?"

"Come on! He's probably getting away right now!"

"Well, I—I—are you absolutely cer-certain, senorita?" he stammered.

"Look, I'm telling you the truth," she said through gritted teeth. "If you don't believe me, come see for yourself."

With a wary sidelong glance at her, the steward slowly climbed the companionway. Nancy was so frustrated, she wanted to scream. Ribeiro would definitely be gone by now!

Sure enough, when they reached Nina's cabin door, it was firmly closed. Although she had little hope of finding anything inside, Nancy made the steward take out his passkey and open the door.

There was no one there. The attacker was gone, and so was Nina da Silva.

The steward made a tiny, formal bow and then hurried back the way he had come. At the end of the corridor he turned and gave her one last dubious look before disappearing. But Nancy wasn't paying any attention to him.

I've got to find Dad and tell him that Mrs. da Silva is gone, she thought. Is he going to freak! Maybe I'd better find out if Captain Brant knows anything first.

She stopped off in her room, just long enough to splash some water on her face, brush her hair, and smooth a little powder blush onto her pale cheeks. No point in letting the world know she was shaken up. Then she tore down to the bridge to speak with the captain.

As she entered the navigation room, Nancy saw that her father was there, talking to Brant. Well, she'd have to tell him sometime. She crossed quickly to his side.

"Dad, hi. Captain Brant. Do either of you know where Mrs. da Silva is?"

Captain Brant frowned. "Funny you should ask," he replied. "As a matter of fact, I just got word that Nina has left the cruise. Looks like she had some urgent business to attend to in the States, so she took a launch ashore this afternoon and caught a flight to Miami. I was about to tell your father."

"Left the cruise!" Carson Drew stared at his friend. "But wouldn't she say something to you before taking off like that?"

Brant shrugged. "I would have expected her to, yes. But Nina's—unpredictable, sometimes. And she's had a lot of business to take care of since Hector died. Maybe it just couldn't wait."

"Even so." Carson shook his head. "I just can't believe she'd go without saying goodbye to—to anyone! Something must have happened."

Nancy took a deep breath. "I think something *has* happened," she told both men. "Mrs. da Silva was being threatened by someone aboard this ship. I'm pretty sure I know who it was, but I'd rather not name him until I know *why* he was threatening her.

"Yesterday morning I overheard a conversation between her and this person," Nancy went on. "She apparently had some sort of map or document he wanted. Badly. She wouldn't give it up. And he told her he had proof about her double-crossing husband."

"What does this all mean?" Captain Brant was looking very confused.

"It means that Mrs. da Silva may well have left in order to shake off a blackmailer. But I don't know what he wanted, or whether he got it."

"Nancy, why didn't you tell me this before?" Carson asked.

"I did tell you, Dad, but you didn't want to hear it."

Carson sighed and rubbed the back of his neck. "I guess I haven't been acting exactly impartial. I'm sorry, honey."

"It's okay." Nancy hugged her father. "No apology necessary."

Captain Brant cleared his throat. "What's our next course of action?"

"There's not much we can do about Mrs. da Silva. She left of her own free will," Nancy pointed out. "But I'd like to investigate on this end, if you don't mind."

"Mind? I was about to beg you to look into it." John Brant looked relieved.

"Good. Now, the first question is, who's in on this? Who told you that Nina was gone?"

Brant blinked. "Why, it was Randy. Randy Wolfe."

Randy Wolfe. What *was* his part in all this? Nancy wondered as she scanned the ballroom for him that evening. What did he know and whose side was he on?

When she heard that Randy had actually known about Mrs. da Silva's departure, Nancy got a sinking feeling in her stomach. He probably knew when they discussed the case that afternoon. Why hadn't he said anything to her? Could Randy possibly be involved with Ribeiro's scheme?

"Nancy, you look fantastic!" Melissa Jordan appeared at Nancy's elbow and nodded approvingly. "What a gorgeous gown—that pink looks great on you."

Nancy smiled. "Thanks, Melissa. You look pretty dazzling yourself. I'm surprised Matt isn't glued to your side."

"Oh, Matt'll be along," Melissa said, bubbling. "I left him figuring out how to tie his own bow tie." She giggled. "Men are so helpless sometimes!"

"Speaking of men, have you seen Randy?" Nancy asked, craning her neck to look around the room.

"Lover boy? I thought you'd had enough of him," Melissa said. "Is this a change of heart? What happened last night?"

"It's a long story." Nancy wasn't about to spill her guts to anyone—she couldn't risk her words getting back to the wrong person. "Nothing interesting happened. And don't worry, I haven't fallen wildly in love with Randy. Far from it. I just want to finish a conversation we were having today." A conversation we *should* have had today, she added to herself.

"Well, here he comes now. And it doesn't look as if you'll have any trouble attracting his attention. My goodness, but that boy certainly is persistent! Excuse me while I fade away!" Melissa gave Nancy a reassuring pat on the shoulder and moved off.

"Blue eyes! You look too gorgeous to be true." Randy threaded his way to Nancy's side and took her hand. "Now I know I didn't slave my afternoon away in vain." He waved his free hand expansively about him. "I planned this whole shebang. What do you think?"

"It's incredible," Nancy said. She wasn't exaggerating. The ballroom had been decorated in green and gold, with huge bouquets of hothouse orchids spilling out of dozens of vases. The moon shone into the room, coaxing rainbows from the many facets of the eight-spoked green glass chandelier that spread across the ceiling.

"Glad you like it. Come on, let's dance!" Randy pulled Nancy toward the double doors leading out to the deck.

"If you're looking for the dance floor, you're going the wrong way," Nancy protested.

"Remember what I said about dancing by moonlight? I'm still working on you, blue eyes."

Nancy sighed. She thought he'd given up. Oh, well, it was a perfect opportunity to have a private talk—if only Randy would listen.

"Did you hear that Mrs. da Silva took off?" she asked casually as they walked along the deck.

She heard Randy draw in his breath. "Yes," he said. Then, abruptly, he turned to face her. "Nancy, I need to talk to you. Let's go someplace where no one can hear." Randy led her aft along the deck, away from the crowd. Nancy felt a twinge of fear. If Randy *was* working for Ribeiro, she'd be putting herself in serious danger. But she had to know what he knew!

Randy threw open the door to the dining room and stood aside for Nancy to pass. Then he closed the door behind them.

Sitting on the edge of a banquette, Randy took Nancy's hand in one of his. "I can tell you that we're dealing with some desperate and ruthless people," he began. "Mrs. da Silva was smart to get out when she did."

He slapped at his neck. "Who'd think there would be mosquitoes this far out to sea?" he grumbled.

"Why? What's she been involved in?" Nancy wanted to stay on the subject. "Stop talking in riddles. Just tell me what's going on!"

"Well," Randy began. Then suddenly he stopped. He gasped, clutching a hand to his neck. "I can't—breathe—"

He slid to the floor, unconscious.

"Randy!" Nancy dropped to her knees beside him. "What's wrong?" She leaned over—and saw a tiny feathered dart, sticking out of Randy's neck!

# Chapter Nine

NANCY GRABBED RANDY'S wrist and desperately tried to find a pulse. She could just feel it, very rapid and very faint under her fingertips.

Still crouching, she scanned the room for signs of an intruder. Her own life could be in danger, too!

But there was no one, no sound, other than Randy's labored breathing and the thudding of Nancy's own heart in her ears.

She couldn't wait any longer. Randy had to have a doctor right away! Jumping up, she ran to the door, yanked it open, and sprinted along the deck to the ballroom.

Spotting her father and Captain Brant amid the crowd wasn't easy, and precious minutes elapsed before she found them.

Pushing her way unceremoniously past several dancing couples, Nancy arrived panting at Carson Drew's table.

"Dad, Captain Brant," she gasped, "no time to explain. Get a doctor and come with me—fast!"

"But wha—" Captain Brant was startled.

"Please—it's a matter of life and death," Nancy spoke quietly, trying to convey the sense of urgency without alerting anyone in the crowd nearby.

The captain made up his mind and nodded. He collected the ship's doctor from a neighboring table and the four of them hurried out.

Nancy raced ahead, arriving at the empty dining room first. As the three men entered, she looked up from where she was checking Randy's pulse again. He was sprawled in an unnatural position, legs folded awkwardly under him. But his heart was still beating!

"Nancy," Carson said as the doctor began to remove Randy's white jacket, "what's going on here?"

"Dad, believe me, if I knew, you'd be the first one I'd tell," Nancy replied ruefully. "All we know is that Mrs. da Silva was being blackmailed—but not for money. It was for something she had, and only she and her blackmailer knew its value.

"When we went to ask her about it, it seemed she might be about to tell us something. That's why it seems so weird that she'd pack up and leave so suddenly. But if her blackmailer found out she was about to talk, maybe he threatened her and she lost her nerve. She seized her chance and left while we were in Paranagua and couldn't stop her."

"But how does Randy figure in this? Does he know anything?" asked Carson Drew, puzzled.

"I don't know. He said he had something to tell me, but then this happened," Nancy explained. "The blackmailer must have overheard Randy telling me he had some information, so he followed us here. Which means that whatever Randy knows, it must be important enough to make some person try to kill him!"

"Well," the doctor said dryly, "whoever it was knew something about South American jungle warfare. This dart is coated with curare, a poison. A little melodramatic but quite effective.

"Luckily, the dosage was weak. See—you can tell by its consistency." He held up a gauze pad with a sticky black smear on it. "The pure stuff is thicker. A dose of that, and our young man would have been dead. I think he'll make it, if we can just get him to the infirmary."

"Thank goodness," Nancy said fervently. She watched as the captain and the doctor carefully lifted Randy's limp body and carried him out.

"Dad, whoever did this wants *me* out of the way, too. Randy and I didn't think that my run-in with the motorcycle was any accident. The rider had on a full helmet—probably to prevent anyone from seeing his face."

Carson Drew nodded and gave a wry smile. "I guess I didn't want to believe there was anything criminal going on, especially if it involved Nina. I am sorry, Nancy."

Together, Nancy and Carson inspected the dining room, looking for any trace of the hidden assailant.

"You know, Dad," said Nancy suddenly, "I don't understand how someone could have shot that dart from inside the room without my seeing him escape. It had to have happened once we closed the door—but I'm almost positive no one was in the room."

"Well, Nan," said Carson, "it was dark, don't forget. There's got to be somewhere he could have hidden. But it's late now. Let's figure it out in the morning."

Nancy still wasn't satisfied, but her father was right. There was nothing more they could do that night. And she did need to get some sleep.

As they left the room, Carson said, "I'm seeing you safely inside your room. This whole thing is starting to make me very nervous."

Nancy laughed. "Oh, Dad, don't worry so much."

Carson Drew sighed. "I'd feel a lot better if we had some tangible evidence to take to the police. This thing is beginning to look like a puzzle with half the pieces missing."

Something clicked in Nancy's brain. A puzzle! What was that note she had received on their first day aboard, if not a puzzle?

"Dad, you're a gem. Here I've had a prime piece of evidence sitting right under my nose, and I didn't see it! I'll check it out and fill you in in the morning!"

Nancy could barely contain her excitement as she unlocked her cabin door. She said good night to her father hastily, closed the door, and ran to her dressing table. She rummaged through her cosmetics case, where she'd tucked the cryptic note with the spider code.

It was gone.

Nancy sat down hard on the bed. She couldn't believe it. The second piece of tangible evidence she'd lost, and it had been practically laid at her feet on the very first day of the cruise!

Strike two, Drew, she said sourly to herself. That spider drawing was somehow crucial to the whole case and you've let it out of your grasp. One more miss, and you're out!

Nancy finally realized that she couldn't just sit there all night. She got up and checked the rest of the room. Nothing else was disturbed.

Going to the cabin door, Nancy opened it and inspected the lock. No sign of forced entry. Well, at least that confirmed her suspicions. Only a crew member would have the master key, so the thief must be employed by the cruise line.

Once more, the facts pointed to Ribeiro.

But again, she couldn't seem to get anything on him. She had no hard evidence.

Nancy stretched wearily. Sitting up all night kicking herself wouldn't help matters. What might help would be a hot bath to relax her.

She opened the bathroom door and reached for the light switch. As she clicked it on, there was a brilliant blue flash. A tingling surge swept up her arm and through her body like a thousand tiny needles.

The shadows in the bathroom grew much deeper all of a sudden. The light spilling in from the bedroom shrank to a tiny point. Nancy's hand felt glued to the light switch. With a great effort, she finally did wrench it free.

Then everything went black.

# Chapter Ten

NANCY AWOKE WITH a start. She was lying on cold, hard tiles and couldn't remember how she had gotten there. Then it came back. Someone had tried to electrocute her!

She tried to get up, but her muscles didn't obey. Her body was tingling, and her legs felt as if they were made of rubber.

With a groan, Nancy struggled to a sitting position on the bathroom floor. She peered at her watch and gasped. It was past one in the morning. She had been there for an hour!

Painfully, Nancy climbed to her feet. Fetching her evening bag from the bed, she shone her tiny flashlight on the bathroom switch. It was surrounded by black scorch marks, and there were deep gouges in the paint where someone had pried it loose to sabotage the wiring.

A long shudder ran down Nancy's spine. So now Ribeiro was playing for keeps! It was sheer luck that she had let go of the light switch before the current did any permanent damage.

Moving shakily, she let herself out of her room and made her way to her father's cabin.

"Nancy!" Carson Drew's face paled when he saw her at his door. "What happened to you?"

"I—" Nancy staggered and Carson caught her. "Someone rigged my bathroom light switch." She tried to smile. "I got a pretty good shock, but I think I'm okay."

*"What?"* Carson exploded. He picked his daughter up and carried her inside, where he placed her gently on his bed and covered her with a blanket. Then he straightened up, his face dark with anger.

"Who did this? How did it happen?" he demanded.

Nancy sighed. "I guess someone broke in during the ball. Everything was fine when I got dressed earlier."

"But *who?*" Carson pressed. "Nancy, do you have any idea who it can be? You've got to tell me!"

Nancy's mind went back to the knife attacker in Mrs. da Silva's room. It had to have been

Ribeiro—but there was something nagging at the back of her mind, some clue that she couldn't quite focus on. She closed her eyes and tried to concentrate, but it was no use. Her head was spinning.

Her father noticed that she looked exhausted. "Well," he said in a gentle voice, "I guess we can talk in the morning. Right now, you'd better get some rest."

He adjusted Nancy's blanket and stretched out in his armchair. Nancy was too tired to protest.

Her body aching, she finally fell asleep.

Nancy had to admit, the world did look a lot better in daylight, after a good breakfast. She reached hungrily for a second piece of toast.

She told Carson her suspicions about Antonio Ribeiro. At first Carson wanted to go straight to Captain Brant, but Nancy pointed out that without any solid evidence, there was nothing they could do. "We need to see what he'll do next," she argued. "He will slip up sometime."

"You're right, of course," Carson grumbled. "But I'm not happy about it."

"Cheer up, Dad. It's a beautiful day," Nancy said with an affectionate grin.

Just then, Captain Brant came over to greet them.

"Captain Brant, how's Randy doing?" Nancy asked quietly.

"Stable, but he's not feeling too well. We'll be transferring him to the naval hospital once we get to Rio," replied the captain. "What's your next move?"

"Well," said Nancy carefully, "I do have one question. Did Antonio Ribeiro go ashore at Paranagua yesterday?"

"Why, no." The captain looked surprised. "He was working on the Rio requisition orders with me almost all day. Why do you ask?"

Nancy sighed inwardly. So Ribeiro couldn't have been riding the motorcycle in Paranagua after all. "Oh, just checking everyone's whereabouts."

She said goodbye and wandered out to the observation deck, where she could just make out Sugarloaf, the cone-shaped mountain that stood high above the Rio de Janeiro harbor.

Just then a scene at the other end of the deck caught Nancy's attention. Antonio Ribeiro was standing with Lynn Ashley, deep in conversation.

Trying to appear nonchalant, Nancy edged closer to the pair. Since there weren't many other passengers on deck, it wasn't easy to get close enough to hear what they were saying.

Ribeiro and Lynn weren't noticing much around them. Lynn was shaking her head vigorously, and Ribeiro appeared to be angry.

Just as Nancy was almost in range, someone

called her name. "Nancy, we've been dying to talk to you!"

Nancy turned to Matt and Melissa Jordan, who looked well rested and fresh in their matching white jogging outfits. Out of the corner of her eye, Nancy saw Ribeiro staring at them with shock. He said something to Lynn and strode away.

Nancy stifled her annoyance and tried to be polite. "So, you two, we'll be landing in Rio in a couple of hours. Are you excited?"

"We are excited, but thought we'd play some killer badminton to pass the time. Care to join us?" Matt asked, in the longest sentence Nancy had heard him utter.

Nancy looked sidelong at Lynn. She was standing and staring out at the ocean with her habitual pout. Nancy didn't see any point in hanging around.

"Sure," she said. Anything to pass the time until we get to Rio and I can *do* something, she added to herself. She was especially anxious to get to a telephone so she could call Ann Granger.

At noon Nancy and Carson joined the other passengers on the Main Deck, watching the Rio harbor draw closer. It was a beautiful sight.

Shimmering in the midday sun was a glass wall of tall luxury hotels, overlooking a broad stretch of white sand. Behind the hotels, a forest of high-rises and tenement buildings sloped up a gentle incline to the real forest—the jungle, just visible in the hazy distance.

Dominating the scene was Sugarloaf Mountain at the city's northern end. A narrow spit of land connected it to the mainland. Nancy could barely make out the two tiny cable cars that were the only way of getting to and from the mountain-top.

As they pulled into the cruiser's berth, Nancy strained her eyes, trying to spot Ned in the waiting crowd. Her attention was caught by two crew members nearby.

"Rio at Carnival!" said one. "What a night this is going to be. I can hear the drums already."

His mate sounded skeptical. "I don't see how we can enjoy ourselves, knowing we have to be back at dawn."

"Yeah," replied the first, "but Captain Brant is a good guy, giving the whole crew shore leave on a night like tonight."

At that moment Nancy caught sight of Ned. He was standing right at the end of the pier, his brown hair shining in the sun. Nancy's heart did its usual flip-flop at the sight of his handsome face and broad shoulders.

She was the first passenger down the gang-plank. Smiling, she twirled into Ned's arms. "Hello, stranger," she said softly.

Ned pretended to look shocked. "Do I know you, miss?"

"Oh, Ned!" Nancy kissed him hard. "Boy, have I missed you."

"All that partying and you still thought of me?" Ned teased gently, as he held her in a bear hug. His warm brown eyes showed how glad he really was to see her.

He shook hands with Carson. Then, grabbing the heaviest suitcase, he led Nancy and Carson to the minibus for the Imperial Hotel on Copacabana Beach, where they would complete their vacation. The cruise ended in Rio.

"Wait till you see this town!" Ned said to Nancy. "People are dancing in the streets—no one can tell *me* Carnival only happens after dark!"

After Carson checked them all into the luxurious hotel suite, Nancy changed into a bright yellow cotton T-shirt, black jeans, and espadrilles and met Ned on the terrace. She wasn't looking forward to telling him she had a new case—she knew he wouldn't be thrilled.

Iced fruit drinks had already arrived when Nancy joined him. "Ned," she began a little nervously, "this isn't exactly going to be one big party."

Ned's grin vanished. "Nancy—you're not on a *case!*"

"Don't be annoyed, Ned," Nancy pleaded. "There's something really strange happening on the *Emerald Queen,* and I've got to find out what it is. Just hear me out."

Nancy quickly outlined the case and the events of the previous three days. "And last night was no joke," she concluded. "Someone means business, and I'm in the way. Which means I must be getting close to some answers!"

"Nancy, I know I'm going to sound like a broken record, but—don't you think this is a matter for the police?" Ned frowned as he looked into Nancy's eyes.

"But what would I tell them?" Nancy gave Ned a pleading stare. "I can't just walk into the Rio police headquarters and tell them someone is playing practical jokes with deadly spiders, or that someone fiddled with my light switch."

"I don't see why not," Ned said.

"I've got to get some hard evidence to give them, or they'll think I'm just a teenager with an overactive imagination. And Captain Brant's reputation may be on the line, too."

Ned looked resigned. "Okay, supersleuth, I might have expected this. So, what do we do now?"

Nancy took a last sip of her strawberry colada and stood up. "First, I've got to call Ann Granger at the *Record.*"

Ann sounded very pleased with herself when Nancy finally got through.

"Nancy, the whole Sea Queen Cruise Line is

wrapped in mystery. Did you ever hear about that South American emerald heist a couple of years ago? The one that happened right there in Rio? . . . Well, Hector da Silva, the owner of the Sea Queen line, was about to be indicted for his supposed involvement in that case when he died. And no one has ever found the loot!"

Nancy's heart pounded with excitement. Da Silva and Ribeiro . . . an unsolved emerald heist . . . a doublecross. . . . At last she began to have an idea what this case was about!

Ann was still talking. Nancy interrupted her friend. "What did they have on da Silva? Was anyone else involved?"

"Well," said Ann, "I checked the line's personnel records—don't ask me how, because I'm not revealing my source. The hotel manager was named Antonio—hold on, I've got it right here—" Papers rustled.

Nancy didn't need to hear the rest. She knew the name would be Ribeiro. "Great stuff, Ann!"

"Do any of these other names ring a bell?" Ann reeled off a few more names. "Avrel, Hinkley, Lopez, Masters, Wolfe—"

"Wolfe! Is that *Randy* Wolfe?"

"You got it," said Ann. "Randall Wolfe, seaman second class. He quit the *Emerald Queen* about a month before da Silva's death."

"Really! Thanks, Ann." So Randy had served on the *Emerald Queen* before! He probably knew a lot more about Ribeiro than he had told her at first. No wonder Ribeiro wanted him out of the way. Well, Randy Wolfe had some explaining to do.

"Ann, I've got to go. Remind me to buy you a deluxe pizza when I get back!"

Nancy hung up the phone. Randy first. She dialed the hospital. After some trouble, she was put through to a supervisor who spoke English.

"Wolfe?" the man's voice replied in answer to her question. "I'm sorry, miss, but we have no American by that name here."

"What?" Nancy was stunned. "Are you sure?"

"Quite sure, miss." The voice sounded annoyed.

Nancy thanked him and hung up. She turned to Ned, alarmed.

"Ned, Randy Wolfe is not in the hospital, which is where he's supposed to be. Do you think something could have happened to him?"

Ned shrugged. "Maybe he discharged himself. It doesn't sound as if he was seriously hurt."

"I hope you're right." Shaking off an uneasy feeling, Nancy went up to her room and changed into sneakers. When she came back down to the lobby, she told Ned, "I hope Randy can take care of himself. Right now we've got to return to the ship."

Nancy started walking briskly toward the door. "I know now what Ribeiro is after—and it looks as if he's just about to find it!"

# Chapter Eleven

"WAIT A MINUTE, Nancy!" Ned finally caught up with Nancy at the lobby doors. He grabbed her by the shoulders and turned her to face him. "What's going on? Why are we rushing out to the ship?"

Nancy grabbed his hand and pulled him along the beach, picking her way between clusters of sunbathers.

"Ned, I promise I'll explain everything to you as soon as we're on our way to the *Emerald Queen,*" she said breathlessly, hauling him toward a minibus stand. "All you need to know right now is that there's a cache of stolen jewels somewhere aboard that ship, and we've got to find it before the bad guy does!"

"Oh, okay, Drew. No problem." Ned grinned at her as they ran. "I can see you've got it under control. Why should I even worry?"

Nancy grinned back. "You've got to admit, life with me is never dull. Oh, hurry, there's the bus!"

"Hey, how do you know this one will take us where we want to go?" Ned asked as the doors slid shut behind them.

Nancy looked sideways at her boyfriend. "I don't exactly *know,*" she admitted with a guilty shrug. "Call it an educated guess."

Ned heaved a deep sigh. "I'm in love with a lunatic," he complained to the ceiling.

Ned and Nancy took seats near the back of the vehicle. Nancy peered out the window at Sugarloaf, which loomed on the right as they whizzed up the avenue toward Rio's city center.

"See?" she chided Ned. "We're going in the right direction. You should trust me. I know what I'm doing."

"Trust you." Ned groaned. "You get into more trouble than anyone I know, Nancy Drew. All right, so tell me what this is all about." He folded his arms and tried to look gloomy. "I just want to know what we're getting into."

"Ann Granger's information filled in a lot of gaps for me," Nancy began. She told Ned about the emerald thefts and Mr. da Silva's indictment.

"So I put that together with what I already knew. One: Antonio Ribeiro was trying to extort some kind of map from Mrs. da Silva. Two: the da Silvas had had serious money problems. Three: Ribeiro and Mr. da Silva had had some correspondence about a map. And then I realized that da Silva must have collaborated with Ribeiro.

"He and Ribeiro together stole this cargo of emeralds somehow and hid it aboard the *Emerald Queen!*"

"Wait a minute—you've lost me," Ned said. "First of all, what makes you think the emeralds are still there? Why didn't da Silva or Ribeiro collect them?"

"Da Silva didn't retrieve them right away, because he was suspected of having stolen them. Then he died before the inquiry was over. And Ribeiro *couldn't* get them, because he didn't know where they were! Da Silva double-crossed him!"

Ned gave a long whistle. "That would certainly explain why he wasn't overly fond of Mrs. da Silva. But where exactly does she fit in? What were you saying about a map?"

Nancy reached over and ruffled Ned's hair. "I'll make a detective of you yet, Nickerson," she teased. "You're asking all the right questions.

"Before he died, da Silva made a map, showing the location of the emeralds. He gave it to his wife so that she'd be able to find them and cash in on them."

"Now, hold on, Nancy," Ned interrupted. "How do you know she hasn't already found them? She could be in Miami living it up!"

"Because she didn't have all the clues!" Nancy replied. "Da Silva wasn't a total crook. He wanted Ribeiro to get his cut. He just wanted to make sure his wife got her share when Ribeiro finally dug them out of their hiding place! He wrote to Ribeiro, telling him that Nina had the key to the emeralds' hiding place. That's the letter I found in Ribeiro's desk.

"But the idea backfired. When Nina came on this cruise, hoping to find the emeralds for herself, Ribeiro tried to intimidate her into giving him the map."

"But she wouldn't," Ned prompted.

"She *couldn't,"* Nancy corrected him. "She couldn't—because she'd already passed the map on to me!"

Doubt shadowed Ned's eyes. "You mean the drawing of the spider? Is that the 'map'?"

"It has to be. At first I thought it was the blueprint of the ship that Ribeiro was after, but then I realized that if it had been anything that simple, Mrs. da Silva would have figured it out and retrieved the emeralds long ago. No, I think that da Silva somehow coded his hiding place in that bizarre drawing, and Mrs. da Silva slipped it under my door. She knew I was a detective. Maybe she hoped that somehow I'd realize what it was and decipher it for her. Or maybe she just lost her nerve and decided to try and hide it from Ribeiro.

"Anyway, I couldn't figure out what the drawing was supposed to mean. I'm hoping Ribeiro hasn't solved it yet."

"So now we have to find the emeralds and get them off the ship before he does." Ned shook his head. "Tall order, Nancy."

Nancy nodded. "Don't I know it." Suddenly she straightened in her seat. "We're here, Ned."

The two teenagers got off the bus and walked along the pier to the cruise ship's docking berth. There wasn't much activity, compared to the morning's bustle. Nancy kept a careful eye out as they walked up the gangplank to the deserted Main Deck. "I'm sure there must be some crew members left on board," she said quietly to Ned.

"Where to?" Ned whispered.

"Upstairs—the Amethyst Deck. Ribeiro's cabin."

"Do you have a credit card?" Nancy whispered to Ned at Ribeiro's door. Ned nodded and handed her a thin plastic card.

"Last time I broke in," Nancy said, smiling as she maneuvered the card between the doorjamb and the tongue of the lock, "all I had was a nail file. These doors are too easy to open, if you ask me." She released the lock and turned the doorknob. "Keep your fingers crossed."

Ribeiro's room was disappointing—they found nothing except business papers. He must have decided to carry his personal papers with him.

Next they tried Randy's room. Maybe, Nancy thought, she'd come across *something* that would tell her what Randy's part in all this was.

Nancy's pulse quickened as she opened the top drawer of Randy's desk. In the back, half hidden under a pile of canceled checks, was a bundle of letters. She started to read the top one.

"Dearest Randy," it began, "how can I ever thank you for making this cruise the best ever for me? . . ." Nancy quickly skimmed the next few letters. All of them seemed to be from old girlfriends.

There was little of interest in Randy's room. "How about trying sick bay?" Ned suggested. "We may be able to learn where they sent him, if he can't be found at the naval hospital."

"Good idea." Nancy nodded. "Let's go."

It was eerie to walk through the deserted corridors. The only sounds were the distant thrum of the ship's engines and their own sneakers softly thudding. Nancy led the way to sick bay, which was aft on the Amethyst Deck. Luckily, there was no one on duty.

But they encountered a snag—the medical logbooks were in a cabinet secured by a combination lock that Nancy couldn't crack.

"Let me try," Ned suggested. He crouched by the lock and cracked his knuckles. In spite of her frustration, Nancy couldn't help but smile.

She got to her feet. "Good luck, Houdini." Looking around the room, she noticed a crumpled white dinner jacket hanging over a chair. She picked it up and examined it. It still had Randy's assistant cruise director nameplate pinned to it. There was a sticky black smear by one of the pockets. It must be curare, from the dart that Randy was shot with.

Nancy frowned. Why did that seem strange?

Just then she heard men's voices in the hall outside. Someone was coming! Quick as a flash, she sprang to the door and locked it.

The voices moved closer, and then Nancy saw the doorknob jiggle. She cast a frantic glance at Ned, who was frozen by the locked cabinet.

"Sorry, sir, I don't have my keys with me," one of the voices said. Nancy closed her eyes in relief. Then the other man spoke.

"Never mind. I'll get mine." The cold tone sent a shiver up Nancy's spine. As both pairs of footsteps moved off, she turned to Ned.

"We've got to get out of here. That was Ribeiro!" she whispered. Ned's eyes widened, and he nodded.

There was no way they could lock the door again once they were outside, but Nancy couldn't worry about that. She grabbed Ned's hand, and they raced up the nearest companionway.

"I just want to get one last look at Mrs. da Silva's cabin," she explained. "Maybe it'll tell me something. I get the feeling Ribeiro's doing the same thing we are. If we don't figure out da Silva's secret soon, he'll beat us to it."

But it was Ned who found it. He'd been feeling around on the upper shelves of the closet, when suddenly Nancy heard him utter a soft exclamation. He turned around, holding a rectangular velvet box in his hands. Nestled in the silk lining was a blaze of gems.

"We found it!" Ned crowed. He drew out a long strand of emeralds in an antique setting and held it up to sparkle in the light.

Nancy grabbed Ned's arm. She'd seen that necklace before! "No, we didn't," she said in a taut voice. "But we *may* have found Mrs. da Silva. Ned, those are her jewels! She'd never have left them behind. Something must have happened to her!"

"Could Ribeiro have killed her?" Ned asked, his voice grim.

Nancy shook her head, her mind racing. "Possible, but I doubt it. She's more useful alive, until he finds the emeralds. No, I think he must be holding her prisoner—and I bet she's somewhere aboard this ship!"

"We'll have to search the whole ship." Ned strode to the door. "Her life's at stake."

Nancy leapt after him. "Ned, that's it! You're a genius! It's got to be."

"What on earth are you talking about?"

"Life! What's the one place on this ship where no one ever goes, except in emergencies? The *life*boats! Follow me!"

Taking the forward companionways so they wouldn't run into Ribeiro, Nancy and Ned dashed down to the Lifeboat Deck. Nancy ran to the railing and scanned the rows of davits. "That one," she said, pointing to a boat that was winched slightly lower than the others.

Together, they raised the lifeboat to the deck. Nancy cleated it into place while Ned rolled back the canvas. She heard him draw in his breath.

"Nancy," he said, "I think we're too late."

# Chapter Twelve

"OH, NO! WE can't be!" Nancy sprang to Ned's side and peered into the lifeboat.

Nina da Silva lay in the bottom of the boat, still and pale as a wax statue. Nancy bit her lip, then reached in and gently pressed a fingertip into the hollow at the base of Nina's throat.

After a moment she looked up at Ned. "She is alive—I can feel her pulse. But it's irregular. And she's so cold! She must be heavily sedated. We've got to get her to a doctor somehow."

"At least she's alive," Ned said, relief evident in his voice. "What are we waiting for?"

Nancy stared. "Do *you* know how we're going

to get Mrs. da Silva down the gangplank in broad daylight, especially in her condition?"

"We don't have to." Ned made a sweeping gesture toward the lifeboat. "Your chariot awaits, m'lady. Step in."

Nancy gaped. "Ned, have you gone—oh, I get it!" She laughed out loud, then clapped a guilty hand over her mouth and stepped quickly into the boat. "Brilliant, Nickerson!" she whispered.

"Call me Houdini." Grinning, Ned climbed in after her. Then he took the hand-operated winch from the boat's locker and attached it to the ropes. As he cranked the handle, the boat sank to the water. Within moments they were afloat.

Nancy and Ned then turned their attention to Nina. "We'll just have to row as close as possible to our hotel in the lifeboat," Ned said. "Then all we have to do is get her onshore, and we're home free."

"The people on the beach are going to be pretty surprised when we come cruising by in a lifeboat," Nancy said.

"We'll just tell them we were up the creek without a paddle. Any idea how to say that in Portuguese?"

Nancy giggled in spite of her concern. He really was wonderful. "I'm beginning to see why I love you, Ned," she said, a smile curving her lips.

"I know—I'm wonderful. Don't worry, I'll

expect payment later. A steak dinner and a walk on the beach should fit the bill," Ned joked.

"Oh, you! Keep quiet and row."

When Ned and Nancy half supported, half dragged Nina into the Drews' suite, Carson jumped from his chair, a frown of concern creasing his face.

"Nina!" He rushed to help with Nina. "What are you doing here? Nancy, what's happened?"

"It's a long story, Dad." Now that she was back in the suite, Nancy suddenly felt bone weary. "Let's get Mrs. da Silva to bed, and then Ned and I'll bring you up to date."

For the next two hours, they discussed the case while Nina slept. Then they ordered a pot of strong Brazilian coffee from room service, and Nancy went into the bedroom and gently woke Nina. Finally, it was time to talk.

The woman was still unsteady on her feet, but she sat upright on the brocade sofa in the suite's living room. Perched on the ottoman facing her, Nancy leaned forward. "So," she said, "where should we start?"

Nina cleared her throat and looked significantly at Ned, wanting him to leave.

Ned was instantly on his feet. "Think I'll go buy a map of Rio," he said, with a let's-humor-her look at Nancy. "I don't want to get lost." He left the suite.

"I suppose I'd better go back to the very beginning," Nina murmured. She stared down at her hands, curled around a steaming cup of coffee, and heaved a deep sigh.

"Hector—my husband—was a good-hearted man," Nina began. "Too good-hearted, one might say. He just didn't seem able to make the hard decisions that businessmen must.

"Hector was once a part owner of the Sea Queen Cruise Line. But things went sour for him. He made some foolish investments, so he sold his share in the business. It almost broke his heart. Hector loved the cruise line. He even accepted the job of general manager aboard the *Emerald Queen,* just so he wouldn't lose contact with his friends and the business.

"Unfortunately, the money we got from the sale soon vanished—Hector had *such* bad luck in the stock market!

"And that, I think, is when Hector got this—this *offer.*" Nina bent her head over her coffee cup again, her shoulders hunched. Nancy shot a quick look at her father. He was watching Nina, his jaw set as though he were afraid of what he might hear.

"Please go on," Nancy said softly.

"Someone told Hector he had access to a cargo of emeralds," Nina continued in a rush. "It was the perfect setup. Hector would hardly have to do anything. This person would steal the emeralds, and Hector, in his capacity as general manager, would hide them aboard the *Emerald Queen* and make sure they got through customs."

"This person you're referring to is Antonio Ribeiro, isn't it?" Nancy asked.

Nina nodded. "Hector never actually told me who his accomplice was, but I knew it had to be Ribeiro. They got to be great friends right around then." She shuddered. "At the time, I didn't understand why.

"Anyway," she continued, "Ribeiro would arrange to sell the gems in Miami, and the two of them would split the profits."

"But then Hector got nervous," Nancy said. "He probably worried that Ribeiro would try to sell the jewels before it was safe. He decided to change the emeralds' hiding place. And then, when he knew he was dying, he thought they might get lost forever. So he sent Ribeiro a letter, saying that you had the map of the new location."

Nina da Silva nodded. "Hector wasn't the sort of man who would betray a friend, no matter what else he might have done."

"Then why did Ribeiro say that Hector was a double-crosser?" Nancy asked.

"He'd slander anyone," said Nina scornfully.

"At any rate, your husband died—suddenly—and no one knew where the emeralds were hidden. Am I right?"

"Yes. . . . Believe me," Nina suddenly burst out, looking at Carson for the first time, "I did try to stop Hector. We needed the money, but I didn't want to get it that way!"

Carson closed his eyes. "I'm not condemning you, Nina," he said quietly.

Nina withdrew for a moment, then turned to Nancy.

"Hector told me about a drawing he had made of the emeralds' location. He was very proud of it—he kept saying that the black widow was the key, but that his 'partner' and I would have to figure it out together. He made it for us, he said. I didn't think about it until I was going through some old papers of his about six months ago." She paused, her eyes lowered.

"You found the drawing of the spider—and you remembered what he had said," Nancy said.

Nina nodded.

"And?" Nancy prompted.

Nina swallowed hard. "And," she echoed, "I decided to find the emeralds for myself. I booked myself on the cruise. But I had no idea where to begin. So when I met you, Nancy, and heard about your—abilities—I realized that I might be able to use you to decipher the drawing for me."

"You slipped it under my door, with a phony note written to make me think it was just a joke puzzle. You figured that I'd work out the code and then tell my dad all about it—and he, of course, would tell you."

Tears welled up in Nina's eyes. "I'm sorry," she whispered to Carson.

Carson rose and strode to the window, where he stood with his back to Nina. "Go on," he said in a tight voice. "I'd like to hear the rest of this."

Nancy felt awful for her dad, but there was nothing she could do or say to help him.

"I was going to tell you everything," Nina moaned. "But Tony Ribeiro wouldn't let me be. I finally told him that I had passed the drawing on to you, but still he kept hounding me. That day when you came to offer me your help—I had decided I needed someone to trust. I couldn't keep up the lies, the evasions. But before I got the chance to speak to either of you, I was attacked."

Nancy stood up and began to pace. "Mrs. da Silva, that's the one thing I don't understand. Why attack you? Why put you out of the way? He had the drawing from my cabin, so he knew as much, if not more than you—"

Nancy broke off. Nina was staring at her, bewildered.

"Did I say Ribeiro attacked me? Oh, no, I'm sorry to have misled you. It wasn't he."

"What?" Nancy was stunned.

Nina shrugged. "Whoever it was put out my cabin lights, but I could tell—even in the dark—that it was someone much smaller than Ribeiro."

"Of course!" Now that Nancy thought about it, her own attacker couldn't have been Ribeiro, either. He hadn't been much bigger than Nancy herself! Her mind racing, she whirled toward Ned, who had just slipped quietly back in. "How could I have missed it?" she asked.

Ned stared back. "Missed what?"

"The obvious. Ribeiro isn't the only one we're up against. He's got an accomplice!"

# Chapter Thirteen

BUT WHO? NANCY thought hard about the person who had held the knife to her throat. It had definitely been a man—she could tell that much in the dark.

What about the masked motorcyclist? The cyclist could have been tall or short, male or female—she just couldn't tell.

"Dad," Nancy said, "think about who went ashore with us at Paranagua. What about Lynn Ashley? Melissa Jordan said she disappeared a couple of minutes after we all split up."

"Nancy," replied Carson Drew reasonably, "I

think a lot of shopkeepers in Paranagua will be willing to vouch for her whereabouts. I just don't see her as a hoodlum."

Nancy was pacing the room, deep in thought. She looked up at Ned, her father, and Nina.

"Don't you all see, something's not adding up here!" she exclaimed urgently. "Whoever this accomplice is, he or she doesn't stop at murder. Look at the rigged switch in my cabin. So why take all this trouble to kidnap Mrs. da Silva and hide her, when they could just as easily have dumped her in the ocean?"

She turned to Nina. "Mrs. da Silva, there must be something else they need, some clue to where the jewels are. Something you have!"

Nina looked bewildered. "I can't imagine what."

Nancy sighed. "Neither can I. But let's take a look at that spider code. Can you help me remember it?"

Together, Nancy and Nina reconstructed the picture of the spider with the tiny letters at each of the eight legs.

When they had finished, Nancy said, "Now, think. Do the letters suggest anything to you?"

Nina looked at the drawing. "Nothing," she said glumly.

"What if we try attaching numbers to each letter?" suggested Ned.

They set to work, using every combination of

letters and numbers they could think of. But they remained stumped.

Nina sighed. "Oh, Nancy," she said wearily, "I've felt for a long time that the answer was right in front of me if I could only see it."

Nancy felt a spark in her mind. She leapt out of her chair. "You did! That's it! It's right in front of you—and everyone else on the ship!"

"Now wait a minute—slow down," said Carson Drew. "What do you mean?"

"Dad, it's the oldest trick in the book!" Nancy's blue eyes sparkled. "How would you hide a fortune in gems from hundreds of passengers who roam freely over a ship?"

"You mean the emeralds are out in the open where everyone can see them?" Ned asked.

"Yes!" Nancy could barely contain her glee. "I'll bet you my whole tape collection they're in the ballroom chandelier, the one with eight spokes, made of green 'crystal'!"

She turned to Nina again. "And you *are* the key. Look again at the letters on the spider's legs." She held up the drawing and pointed. "See? *A, W, N, P, I, Y, N,* and *F*. That's clockwise. But if you go the other way"—she traced her finger counterclockwise—"there's your name: *N-I-N-A,* spaced out to every other letter. That must indicate the location of the emeralds."

"Well," said Carson Drew, "it seems we've finally got a case to take to the Rio police."

"No," said Nancy. "That's exactly what we don't have. We need material evidence. We don't have much time; we sail at dawn. The police will take too long.

"And I want to get *them,* not just the jewels. Remember, they've tried to kill me three times, and I'm starting to take it personally!"

"I'm with Nancy, Mr. Drew," said Ned. "We can't wait."

Nancy felt a surge of relief and affection for Ned. Much as he sometimes disagreed with her methods, he always came through.

She got to her feet. "It's a little after seven now—it'll be dark in a half hour or so. I think we should go back on board then.

"Let's leave now, Ned, and walk to the docks. We can pick up something to eat on the way—I'm starving!" Nancy's stomach rumbled, and she blushed. Ned laughed.

Nancy went into her room and grabbed a black sweatshirt to wear over her bright T-shirt. She made sure her penlight was in her jeans pocket. "Okay, let's roll," she called.

Carson Drew walked them down to the lobby. "John's expecting the three of us to join him for dinner at the restaurant on top of Sugarloaf later." He chuckled hollowly. "Won't he be surprised when I show up with Nina instead?"

"Dad—" Nancy put her hand on her father's arm. "I'm really sorry it turned out this way."

Carson straightened his shoulders. "Ah, well," he said, walking away.

"Cheer up, Nancy," said Ned softly behind her. "You did the only thing you could under the circumstances. Besides, wouldn't it be a lot worse if your father found this out after they got really close?"

"I know," said Nancy sadly.

Ned put his arm around Nancy's shoulders. "Come on. They'll work it out themselves. Now let's get some food—we've got work to do!"

Fifteen minutes later, moving through the gaudily dressed crowds that filled the streets of Rio, Nancy did feel better. They had picked up Brazilian beef kebabs from a street vendor, and now her attention was mostly occupied with holding onto her kebab with one hand and Ned with the other. She didn't want to lose either in the mob.

And it *was* a mob. Nancy had never seen anything like it. Drumbeats filled the air with a frenzied tattoo, and the whole city seemed to be dancing to its rhythm.

Already many in the crowd were dressed in costume for the night's Carnival festivities. As the evening darkened into night, torches appeared as if from nowhere, casting an eerie glow in the sequined and feathered processions.

They arrived at the docks. Nancy looked up at the bulk of the *Emerald Queen* looming above them. "I feel like we're going on a commando raid," she said with a nervous laugh.

Ned didn't laugh. "Just be careful, Drew," he said and hugged her. They climbed the rope ladder single file.

Keeping close to the shadows, Nancy led Ned up the five short companionways. They stopped in front of the darkened ballroom. Nancy pushed one of the heavy glass double doors slowly open.

She played her penlight on the ceiling of the huge room. "That's where the emeralds are," she whispered.

"Nancy, how are we going to reach that chandelier? It must be sixteen feet in the air!" Ned gasped as it became clear what Nancy meant.

Leaving Ned in the shadows, Nancy went to the tables at the edge of the dance floor. After dragging one out to a position directly under the giant chandelier, she placed a tall bar stool on top of it and centered it carefully. She secured it with two chairs to keep it from toppling over. Then she climbed her homemade ladder.

Nancy knew that every *other* spoke of the chandelier contained emeralds instead of crystal, but she had no way of knowing where the sequence started. The hundreds of dangling green teardrops looked exactly alike. Da Silva must have planned this very carefully.

But wait. The emeralds would be much harder than the crystal—Nancy remembered that much from geology. She pulled out her nail file—how useful it had turned out to be!—and gently scratched at one of the pear-shaped stones with the file's tip.

The sharp point moved over the surface of the stone without leaving a mark.

It was a genuine emerald.

Stifling an urge to shout the good news to Ned, Nancy let out some of her excitement in an explosive sigh.

" 'Welcome to my parlor,' said the spider to the fly."

Antonio Ribeiro's voice came from an open floor-to-ceiling window opposite the doors.

As Nancy's eyes focused slowly in the darkness, she saw the cold gray barrel of a gun.

# Chapter Fourteen

RIBEIRO BEGAN MOVING slowly toward Nancy, a cruel smile twisting his face.

"Miss Drew, you simply don't know what a pleasure it is for me to have you as my special guest at last," he said smugly. "You've led me quite a dance, you realize.

"But it's all been worth it. And now that you've shown me where the emeralds are, I regret that we must say goodbye. Please come down here."

Nancy descended slowly. "I hope you don't think you can use that gun on me and get away with it," she replied coolly. "You'd have the

American consulate on your tail within minutes."

Ribeiro wasn't moved. "On the contrary, Miss Drew. I've got the entire ocean at my disposal for getting rid of your body. And even if they traced your movements to this ship, we could be in another country by then, and South America doesn't necessarily care about extraditing people to the United States. And, even were I caught and charged with your death, I could say I shot an unknown intruder in self-defense."

Nancy wondered wildly where Ned was. It looked as if Ribeiro didn't know she had a companion on the ship. Playing for time, she asked, "Why did you kidnap Mrs. da Silva?"

"Kidnapping is not one of my vices. Nina da Silva may not be the world's brightest woman, but at least she had the sense to get out of my way and leave the cruise."

Suddenly, a tall dark figure came flying out of the shadows. Ned!

The hotel manager's right arm flew into the air as the gun went off. His bullet whizzed past Nancy's head and shattered a window on the far side of the room.

Nancy started forward to help Ned as he and Ribeiro grappled. "Look out!" she cried. Ribeiro was about to club Ned with the heavy gun butt.

Ned twisted aside, and the two of them crashed to the floor amid a pile of barstools.

They broke apart. Nancy bit her lip as she tried to see what was happening. Then Ned staggered to his feet.

"Come on, Ned," Nancy yelled. "He's still got the gun!"

The two teenagers ran for the open deck. By the time they got to the companionway, Nancy could hear footsteps pounding behind them. And the gangway was still five decks below them!

Nancy's brain was moving as fast as her feet. Ribeiro obviously didn't know that someone had kidnapped Mrs. da Silva! If he wasn't involved in that, then was it possible that he wasn't the mastermind here?

Nancy and Ned clattered down the last companionway. The gangplank was just in front of them. As they raced across the open deck, another bullet whistled through the air.

"Get down, Nancy!" Ned shouted. He grabbed her hand, and together they rolled down the gangplank.

"Keep going!" gasped Nancy as they hit the ground. "Head for that crowd—he won't dare shoot at us there."

Nancy and Ned dashed across the wharf, ducking in and out of the shadows cast by the huge ships. She cast a quick glance over her shoulder at the *Emerald Queen.*

No one. Nancy didn't like that. Ribeiro couldn't have given up so easily. And if he was chasing them, she would have preferred to know where he was.

They crossed a broad avenue, and Nancy began to breathe a little easier. Maybe Ribeiro had given up after all—in which case there was still work to be done!

"Ned, I don't know how much you heard back there," she said, "but if Ribeiro wasn't lying, he didn't even know Mrs. da Silva was kidnapped!"

Ned nodded. "Yeah, I caught that," he replied. "So that must mean Ribeiro and his accomplice aren't telling each other everything."

"Yes, and I'm not sure I like that. If this accomplice has some initiative, that makes him or her that much more dangerous. All right, here's the plan."

Nancy hated to split up, but she saw no other way. "You've got to go back and keep an eye on the emeralds. I'll go up to Sugarloaf to get Captain Brant. The police may not listen to me, but they will listen to *him.*"

Ned nodded reluctantly. "Okay, boss lady. But you'd better be careful. Ribeiro's bound to figure out where you're headed, and he might be desperate enough to come after you."

"Oh, Ned." Nancy put her arms around him and kissed him. "*You're* the one who should be careful. I'm giving you the dangerous job. I'm sorry."

"I'll be fine." Ned smiled into her eyes, and Nancy tried to swallow her uneasiness.

They parted, diving into the festive crowd, and Nancy began to thread her way toward the cable-car landing.

This isn't going to be easy, she thought after several breathless minutes. The crowd was so dense that it could take hours to reach the landing.

Dodging a drunken reveler, Nancy headed for a side street. She'd have to take a detour. It was better than trying to get through a solid mass of people.

The narrow alley she found herself in was less crowded, but by no means clear. The air was still and heavy away from the waterfront, and Nancy peeled off her sweatshirt. Taking a deep breath, she shoved her way past a crowd of masked children.

Several minutes later Nancy realized she had dropped her sweatshirt. With nothing but her bright yellow cotton T-shirt on, she was starting to feel chilled.

What was worse, she was lost, hopelessly lost. Taking all the side alleys to avoid the crowds, she had completely lost her sense of direction. And Ned had the map.

She stopped at a newsstand to catch her breath and ask for directions. *"Por favor, una mapa,"* Nancy tried in Spanish.

The fat proprietor looked at her stonily. *"No mapa,"* he said. He obviously didn't appreciate having to work while everyone else went to Carnival, and he was going to let Nancy know about it.

*"Importante!"* Nancy added in desperation. She had to get to Sugarloaf—and fast.

The shopkeeper stared at her and, grunting with the exertion, reached a grubby map from one of the dusty upper shelves.

Nancy figured she was about ten minutes away from the cable-car landing. At least she hadn't gone too much off the track in her wandering.

"Thanks!" she yelled over her shoulder at the sullen shopkeeper as she left the dingy store.

As she moved into the street, she caught sight of a figure in a white uniform out of the corner of her eye. Ribeiro! He had found her somehow! Nancy cursed her luck. She'd have to lose him and hope that he didn't figure out where she was going.

Nancy ducked around a corner and found herself in the midst of a garish group of dancing people. She crouched under the wing of a large man dressed like a bird and managed to stay hidden in the group as they moved through the street, dancing and singing.

But when they turned up a wide avenue, which would take Nancy away from the landing, she left their protecting numbers and hurried forward.

Head down, she fought her way through the surging mass of people. She seemed to be the only one heading for the cable cars—everyone else was going to the center of town.

Not looking carefully, Nancy ran smack into someone. She tried to raise her head but could only stare at a white ship's uniform. Strong arms seized her and pinned her arms to her sides.

Now I'm dead! thought Nancy.

# Chapter Fifteen

NANCY STRUGGLED, TRYING to break free. Then, suddenly, she was released and looked up.

"Hey, blue eyes, what's the matter? You look like you just saw a ghost!"

Nancy stared. "Randy!" she gasped. "What are you doing here?"

"Why do you keep asking me that? It's fate, pure and simple. Now, more to the point, what are *you* doing here? Is someone chasing you?"

"Ribeiro. I thought you were Ribeiro. I thought I was about to be killed!"

"You've figured something out!" Randy's

green eyes gleamed with excitement. Surprised, Nancy stared at him.

"How did you guess that?" she asked.

"No guessing, Watson. Deduction," Randy said smoothly. "Why else would he bother to chase after you? You either have something that he wants, or you know something he doesn't want you to. Right?"

"Impressive!" Nancy raised her eyebrows. "You're absolutely right. I figured out what he's been looking for. It's a cache of emeralds that he and Mrs. da Silva's husband stole together. I know where they are. Unfortunately, so does Ribeiro."

Randy grabbed her arm. "You know where they are?" he cried. The passing crowd turned, looking interested. Randy grimaced and pulled Nancy into the shelter of a shop doorway. "Have you seen them?" he went on in a lower voice. "Where are they?"

Nancy pulled her arm away. Suddenly, she felt acutely uneasy. Why was he so excited? "Randy," she said, making it into a joke, "it sounds as if you've got a vested interest in those emeralds yourself."

"Me?" Randy threw back his head and laughed. "Come on, Nancy! I've just never been close to that much money before. It's natural curiosity. But you don't have to tell me if you don't want to. So where were you running to just now?"

Maybe it *was* just natural curiosity. "Up to the restaurant on Sugarloaf," Nancy told him. "Captain Brant's up there, with Dad and Mrs. da Silva."

"Mrs. da Silva's back? Well, well. Want company?"

Nancy didn't. "Um, actually, Ned and I got separated," she improvised, "and I've got to find him first. Guess I should try the hotel."

"I'll go with you," Randy said, taking her arm again. "You might need the protection."

"Wait a minute!" Nancy cried. She was getting more and more uneasy. "Randy, you still haven't answered my question. What *are* you doing here? Why aren't you in the hospital?"

"I never checked in," Randy said, shrugging. "I was feeling fine. Whoever tried to kill me with that dart miscalculated his dosage. Curare can be lethal in concentrated form, but when diluted, it works as a muscle relaxant. There was only enough on the dart to relax me—all the way to unconsciousness." He grinned, rubbing his neck reminiscently.

Bong! Alarm bells started going off in Nancy's head. Why hadn't she seen it earlier?

She flashed on Randy slapping at a mosquito as they walked into the deserted dining room. Then on herself in sick bay, holding Randy's dinner jacket. The curare on the lip of the pocket—like the smear on Nancy's hand when she'd touched the dart. That stain on

Randy's jacket pocket could mean only one thing.

Randy must have been carrying the dart in his pocket and then stuck it into his neck while pretending to slap at a mosquito. The curare had taken effect quickly, and within five minutes Randy was unconscious. No wonder Nancy hadn't been able to figure out where the shot could have come from. It hadn't come from anywhere at all.

Randy had drugged himself!

It was all clear. The letter to *R*, the things Ribeiro should have known about but didn't, the doublecross that Nina da Silva denied . . .

He must have drugged himself to divert my suspicion from him, Nancy thought. And he's been manipulating me from the start.

Nancy suddenly realized Randy was after her, and that realization must have shown on her face because Randy was gazing quizzically at her. "What's up?" he asked. "Something wrong?"

"Uh—no," Nancy said quickly. "I just remembered something I have to do. Look, Randy, I'll be fine on my own. And you really can't be feeling so great yet."

"Don't worry about me," Randy reassured her. "I can keep up!"

"No!" Nancy said quickly. She had to think fast. "I mean—well, to tell you the truth, Ned's jealous. I don't think he'll be happy to see me with you."

There was a pause, then Randy shrugged. "Well, okay," he said.

"See you later!" Nancy waved and walked away. Her knees were shaking, but she managed not to let it show.

Where to first? she wondered. The police won't believe me if I tell them this story. I don't have any evidence! No, I've got to get up to Sugarloaf —it's the only option. Randy might even go there himself, now that he knows we've found Mrs. da Silva. They could be in real danger. I'll just have to beat him there!

Nancy began to walk toward the dark mass of Sugarloaf's cone.

She stopped on a street corner to let a procession of yellow-robed people go by. Probably members of a religious sect, she guessed. As they marched, they chanted an eerie dirge, punctuated with heart-rending wails. Nancy tapped her foot impatiently against the curb, waiting for them to pass.

When they had finally gone by, Nancy ran across the street to a man who was selling noisemakers from a big cardboard box.

She was about to ask him for directions to Sugarloaf when, mirrored in a darkened shop window, she caught a flash of white in the crowd. She spun around, and saw a man in a ship's uniform. His cap of sun-streaked golden hair glowed in the light of a street lamp. As she stared, he grinned knowingly at her.

It was Randy. He was following her.

Nancy's blood hammered in her ears. So he knew she knew. I should have guessed something was up when he let me go so easily, she realized.

Now he not only knew where Nancy was headed, but it was getting pretty obvious he had something in mind—something special for her. He was trying to scare her by following her. Nancy had to admit he was doing a good job.

She must stand out like a beacon in her bright yellow T-shirt. What an idiot she was to have lost her sweatshirt! She could have kicked herself. How could she escape him?

Then, looking down at her shirt, Nancy had a sudden inspiration.

Putting on a burst of speed, she raced down the block, turned left, ran down another block, turned left again, and slowed to a rapid walk. There—she had doubled back and was retracing her own steps. Now she had to get someplace where her yellow blouse wouldn't advertise her presence.

After another minute or two, Nancy caught sight of the little yellow-robed band as it wended its way toward the bay.

She hurried forward, pausing for a moment to snatch a gaily colored square of cloth from an old woman who was waving it in the air. Nancy pressed a handful of coins into the old woman's outstretched palm. "Thanks!" she called as she began to knot the cloth around her reddish gold hair. Then she ran on, turning once to see the old woman staring after her, mouth agape.

Pushing and ducking, Nancy made her way to the heart of the group of chanters. Not one of them seemed to notice her arrival. So far, so good. With her black jeans out of sight, her hair covered, and her yellow shirt matching the chanters' robes, it would be almost impossible for anyone on the sidewalk to spot her.

When she dared to look up at the crowds, Randy was nowhere in sight. She was surprised to see that her group had crossed a wide boulevard already, and was almost at the end of the bay, where the waterfront gave way to the beach. Sugarloaf towered on her left. She'd made it.

Nancy detached herself from the group and jogged down the curve of the beach to the cable-car landing, pulling off her headscarf as she ran. She knew she was conspicuous against the white sand, but she couldn't worry about that now. She just had to get up to the top of the mountain.

The landing was deserted. One car sat in the loading bay; the other must be up at the top already. Nancy knocked on the door of the lighted switch booth, and a tiny elderly man opened it and looked suspiciously at her.

"Please—I have to get to the restaurant," she said.

The operator didn't move. Pulling out some money, Nancy pressed it into his hand, pointing up the slope and then at herself in hopes that he would understand the urgency of her gestures.

"Car leaves in ten minutes," the man said suddenly.

So he did understand her! "This is an emergency," Nancy said. "I know it's inconvenient, but please—people's lives may be at stake!"

"Car leaves in ten minutes," he repeated. "We wait for more passengers."

Nancy wanted to scream. Time was ticking away. Randy could be here any minute! She tried again. "Look, I'll pay you for your time," she offered. "I've got a traveler's check right here."

The operator looked over Nancy's shoulder, off into the distance. "Okay, get in," he finally said. "Pay up top." He waved her toward the cable car.

"Thank you very much," Nancy said fervently. She opened the door and climbed into the car. The operator stood by the switch in a waiting attitude.

Impatiently, Nancy leaned out the window. "Hey, what are we waiting for?" she called.

The operator looked at her as if she were a little slow on the uptake. "Other passenger," he explained in a patient voice.

Other passenger! "But you just said—" Nancy

began. She never finished the sentence. She didn't have to.

Her question was answered for her as the doors shut behind the other passenger, who'd just climbed on board.

It was Randy Wolfe!

# Chapter Sixteen

NANCY LUNGED FOR the door, but Randy was too quick for her. He stepped in front of it and barred the way with his hands. "What's your hurry, blue eyes?" he said, mocking her.

Nancy spun around, filling up her lungs to scream. Maybe there was still time to get the cable-car operator's attention! But her scream was cut short, coming out as a muffled squeak, as Randy caught her around the waist and, with a sharp blow to her midriff, sent the breath whooshing out of her.

Through a haze of pain, Nancy could see the car operator watching them. Randy still held her in a close embrace. She moved her leg to kick him, but he stomped viciously on her foot, drawing an involuntary groan from her.

Pinning her arms behind her back with one hand, Randy raised his other to give the operator a reassuring wave. To Nancy's horror, the man waved back, then disappeared into his booth. She was on her own!

"He thinks we've just patched up a lovers' quarrel," Randy murmured, his mouth stretching in a ruthless grin. It distorted his handsome face, making him look like a hungry shark.

"Ah, ah—no tricks," he cautioned as Nancy tensed for a karate kick. He shook his sleeve, and a switchblade dropped into his palm. He clicked it open and held the point to the corner of Nancy's jaw. "I'm sure you remember this little toy."

"You won't get away with this, you know," Nancy said through clenched teeth. "Murder is a heavy charge, Randy, and you're going to have an awfully hard time explaining my corpse to my father once we arrive at the restaurant." There was a hum of electricity. Suddenly the lights flickered on, and the car began to lurch out of the loading bay. Nancy fought down fear. "Why don't you quit while you're ahead?"

There was a dull thud outside—on the roof?—and the car rocked heavily from side to side, banging against the concrete lip of the platform.

Nancy couldn't control her start. She peered at the windows, trying to see what was outside, but the darkness turned the lighted car into a huge mirrored box. Everywhere she looked, all she could see was Randy's face!

His knowing leer broadened. "These cable cars are not too safe," he said nastily. "Rickety as old tin cans. People say it's as much as your life is worth to ride this line—the couplings are so rusty that a good strong breeze could knock these cars right off the cable. Now, wouldn't that be a tragic accident?"

A sick feeling grew inside Nancy, but she forced herself to speak calmly. "No matter what you do to me, Randy, you're through. Ned knows everything, and he's already gone to the police."

"You're trying to bluff me," Randy sneered. "But it won't work. I know you didn't get a chance to speak to Ned after we met up, and I know he won't put all the pieces together like you did. He's not as smart as you, blue eyes. You know, you *are* very intelligent. I like your style. A smart little snoop. Too bad it's going to get you killed."

"Even without me, the emeralds are already out of your reach," Nancy lied. If she could only keep him talking long enough, maybe she could form some plan to get herself out of this mess! "Ned has material evidence. Oh, yes, we retrieved an emerald, did I forget to tell you? The police are probably heading out to the *Emerald*

*Queen* right now. By the time you get there, they'll have confiscated everything of value. Unless you have a plan to stop them?" She put a deliberately contemptuous tone into her question.

Randy's grin faltered for an instant, and the point of the knife jerked against Nancy's jaw, making her gasp.

"Sorry about that," Randy murmured. He laughed without humor. "You shouldn't try to upset me, you know. It isn't healthy.

"As for the police," he went on, his voice growing sure again, "I'm not worried about *them.* There's a Carnival going on here, didn't you notice? It's the biggest holiday of the year, and if I know Rio—and I do—the cops will be out whooping it up with everybody else. Your *boyfriend"*—he laid an unpleasant stress on the word—"isn't likely to find anyone at home when he calls in at precinct headquarters."

A cold fist closed around Nancy's heart. For the first time, she felt the approaching chill of despair. What if she couldn't fool Randy?

Snap out of it, Nancy! she berated herself. There's always a chance. Just keep him talking—as long as he talks, *you* stay alive.

She forced her muscles to unknot a little. Randy's grip tightened around her waist. She gave him a pained look. "You're hurting me," she complained. "Can I sit down?"

"Poor thing," Randy taunted her, but he did

let go of her waist. Just as quickly, though, he grabbed her thick hair and twisted his hand in it, pulling her head back. "All right, sit."

He's trying to intimidate me any way he can, Nancy realized. He's worried that I might try to escape, so he's making sure I don't believe I can. Which means that he isn't so sure of himself as he seems! Maybe I can use that.

Sitting up as straight as she could with his grip on her hair, Nancy looked at Randy's reflection in the window of the car and let a little smile play on her lips. "So tell me," she said. "How did you do it all? The box full of black widows in Mrs. da Silva's room—the note with my flowers—the 'accident' that was no accident in Paranagua—it must have been a lot of work."

Randy smirked. "Grunt stuff. The menial work. I let Tony Ribeiro handle most of those details, which, by the way, was a mistake I'm not going to repeat. He almost blew everything, the idiot. If he hadn't threatened the da Silva woman and made her suspicious, I would've been able to charm that drawing out of her. And if he hadn't messed up the early attempts to get rid of you, I wouldn't have to bother with you now."

"Why did you save my life at Paranagua?" Nancy couldn't help asking.

Randy frowned. "That motorcycle was Tony's idea. He hired a local to run you down and didn't even tell me until after all the arrangements were made. But I'm the boss—I'm the one calling the shots around here! So I screwed up his plan to teach him a lesson. He had to learn that no plan could work without my say-so."

"I see," Nancy commented dryly. She was thinking, Boy, this guy sure has delusions of grandeur! Why didn't I notice it before?

"Besides, it was too obvious," Randy was saying. "All of Tony's plans were too obvious—which isn't going to look very good at his trial, you know. Those attempted murders can all be traced to him. But my tracks are covered. Who's going to believe him when he tries to point the finger at me? Nobody. And that means a nice long jail term for him and a big, fat stack of money for me."

"So you'd sell out your own partner," Nancy muttered.

"Welcome to the real world," Randy said softly. He chuckled. "Would you like to hear what happens now?"

Nancy's mouth went dry. Was this it?

"Don't worry, blue eyes," Randy taunted as he saw her fear. "You've still got a few more minutes. "I'm talking about what happens to your dear old dad and the charming widow when I tell them that you sent me because you're in trouble and couldn't come yourself. I'm talking about what happens when we three get into this car, and the coupling begins to go, and I go up on the roof to check it out."

Nancy gasped. He was going to kill her father and Nina, too!

"You see, there's a particularly nasty spot down there on the ground below us, where a bunch of sharp rocks stick up out of the grass. And if anyone fell onto those rocks from this height, car or no car, they'd be killed instantly."

Crack! There was a sharp report on the roof. At that instant, the lights in the cable car winked out. Now or never! Nancy thought, and shot straight up from her seat to butt Randy in the chin with her head.

Randy let go of her hair and reeled backward, cursing. Without thinking, Nancy threw herself forward, trying to knock the knife from his hand.

Even as Nancy twisted and rolled, Randy tightened his grip on the knife. She dove for it but barely missed. She slammed against the floor with her left shoulder and lay there dazed for a second.

It was one second too long. Randy tackled her, slapping the knife against her neck. A low growl of rage came from his throat as he dragged her to her feet and pushed her back into the seat.

"So you want to play rough, huh?" Randy panted. Out of breath, Nancy didn't answer. She'd need all the help she could get. He was insane!

Randy shook her, his mouth twisted in a horrible imitation of a grin. His teeth gleamed in the moonlight.

Randy paused. In the moment of stillness, Nancy heard the roof creak again. It almost sounded as if there was someone up there. If only!

"Well, playtime's over. No more fun and games," Randy said in her ear. Turning her around, he shoved her so that she stumbled over to the doorway.

Without warning, Randy reached over and unlatched the door. Realizing what he meant to do, Nancy aimed a desperate kick at his knife hand, but he danced out of her way. "Bon voyage, Nancy Drew," he whispered.

Then he pushed her out!

# Chapter Seventeen

As Nancy started to fall, she grasped desperately at the cable car, twisting her body in the air. As her right hand closed around something that stuck out from beside the door, she felt a searing pain in her right shoulder.

But she wasn't falling anymore. She had grabbed one of the safety rails on the outside of the cable car.

With a stifled groan, she brought her left hand up to grip the bar. Her right shoulder throbbed agonizingly, but she was alive—and determined to stay that way.

Randy was standing with his back to her at the

front of the car, enjoying the view of the approaching mountain.

Nancy began a slow, excruciating hand-over-hand climb up the vertical rail. If only she had enough strength to hoist herself up to the roof of the car before Randy turned around!

With a shudder, Nancy clenched her teeth and reached for a higher grip on the bar.

Suddenly, her blood froze. Her hand wasn't holding the metal of the bar anymore. It had been grasped by a human hand!

"I've got you, Nancy," came a whisper from above.

Nancy looked up. It was a miracle—Ned! He must have climbed on the roof before the car left the landing! It had been his weight swaying the car.

Blinking back tears of relief, Nancy managed to squeeze Ned's hand. His grip tightened on hers reassuringly. Then he reached down and grabbed her aching right arm.

Nancy tried to stifle her yelp of pain, but it was too late. Randy had heard her. He turned, surprised, and saw Nancy hanging in the open doorway of the cable car.

His face split in a cruel smile as he said, "My detective friend, lovely as you are, you are really becoming quite a pest."

He started toward the door, the knife glinting in the moonlight.

"Oh, no you don't!" Nancy said between

clenched teeth. Knowing Ned had her firmly by both hands, she ignored the tearing in her shoulder as she kicked out and back with her full weight.

Nancy aimed her kick at Randy's stomach and, just as he struck out with the knife, she caught him with both feet squarely in the solar plexus.

Clutching at his stomach and gasping for breath, Randy lost hold of the knife as he fell backward. He hit his head sharply on the edge of a seat and lay still.

The knife skittered across the floor of the car and fell, spinning, into the darkness below.

Ned began to haul Nancy up, inching back on his belly across the top of the car. When he tugged on her right arm, she saw white stars. She clenched her teeth as he slowly pulled her up and over, grunting with the effort. There was a terrifying moment when she thought he was going to drop her, but at last they lay panting on the roof.

"Ned, how in the world—"

"Shh. Don't talk." Ned drew her into his arms and held her for a long moment.

"Just how did you end up on the roof?"

"I'm only sorry I couldn't get in there to help you, but this door is stuck," he said, pointing to the rooftop emergency hatch.

"After I went back to the ship, Ribeiro came

back, too. I was hiding under the gangplank, and he walked right over my head! And he wasn't alone! So I tagged along. Well—" Ned broke off as they heard Randy stirring below them.

Nancy figured out how to release the catch on the emergency hatch and they scrambled down through the opening.

Randy Wolfe was rubbing his head, attempting to sit up. When he saw Ned and Nancy leaping down on him, he tried to stand, looking wildly around for his knife.

"You won't be needing that knife where you're going!" Ned cleared the two yards between them in one jump and locked Randy in a full nelson.

"Better give up, Randy," Nancy advised the struggling man.

"You two think you've got something on me?" Randy asked as Nancy tied his legs together with her belt. "Well, think again!" Randy's face was red, and his eyes bulged with rage. "Who's going to believe some harebrained girl detective and her muscle-headed boyfriend?"

"Well, for starters, them." Nancy pointed to her father, Nina da Silva, and Captain Brant waiting at the mountaintop cable landing with a few others.

"What happened? Who's in there—Nancy! Are you all right?" Carson Drew impatiently pulled the doors open just as the car arrived.

"Carson was looking out the window and saw

the lights go out, and people on top of the car, and he realized something was wrong," Captain Brant put in.

Nancy ran to her father and gave him the biggest hug her shoulder would allow.

"You have no idea how glad I am to see you!" Nancy felt the tension of the last few minutes—it seemed like hours!—falling away from her, and she clung to her father for a moment.

Then she pointed to Ned, who was holding the now sullen and disheveled Randy in a wrestler's grip.

"I think we can call the police now," she said quietly.

# Chapter Eighteen

I'M TELLING YOU, you could have knocked me over with a feather!" Matt Jordan said, shaking his head admiringly.

It was the next morning, and Ned, Nancy, Carson, and the Jordans were gathered on the terrace in front of the Imperial Hotel for a late breakfast. The Jordans had been at the restaurant by chance the night before, and Matt was so excited about what had happened that for once he couldn't seem to stop talking.

He went on, "When Melissa and I came out to the landing, and we saw the police arriving to take Randy away, and then Captain Brant said that Randy tried to kill Nancy, well . . ."

Matt trailed off, his ears turning red as he realized everyone at the table was listening to him.

"It was like a movie!" Melissa picked up the end of her husband's sentence. "I mean, just think about it! Here's Nancy, the beautiful young undercover agent—"

"Let's not get carried away, Melissa," Nancy interrupted, laughing.

"Nancy, you've got to let me tell this story right." Melissa shook her fork at Nancy in mock severity. "Although why I'm still friends with you, when you never once let on that anything funny was going on—even when we asked you! —is beyond me."

"Hey, give me a break!" Nancy reached for the platter of fried plantains. "I didn't know *what* was going on. At one point I suspected practically everyone on the ship of being involved in some huge conspiracy! For all I knew, you two could have had a cabin full of black widow spiders, just waiting to be used on your victims."

*"Us?"* Melissa shrieked. "Nancy Drew, I can't believe you thought that about us."

As Nancy opened her mouth to protest, Melissa waved her to silence. "I don't want to hear it. I've had enough. I don't want to hear another word from you."

Then the twinkle in Melissa's dark eyes gave her away. "Unless, of course, you want to tell us what really *did* happen," Melissa added, grinning conspiratorially at Matt.

"Well, as I said, for a long time I was really in the dark myself," Nancy began. She told them about the chocolate box full of spiders, and the conversation she had overheard on the Pearl Deck, and the attempts on her own life.

"So, from the very first day of the cruise, I knew there was something wrong aboard the *Emerald Queen*. But no one else seemed to think so."

Nancy sneaked a glance at her father. Nina da Silva had caught an early flight to Miami that morning, after Carson had seen her off.

"Nancy means *I* was being a little thick-headed," he put in. "Which is very true. I couldn't see the forest for the trees." Carson Drew's eyes were tired and a little sad, but he smiled at his daughter anyway.

"See, the confusing thing about this case was that for the longest time all I had was a bunch of suspects," Nancy went on. "Here were all these people acting very much like criminals, but I couldn't see that any crime was being committed."

"There *was* no crime, right?" Ned asked. "I mean, the actual crime—the emerald heist—happened a year ago."

"Exactly." Nancy nodded and took a sip of

coffee. "Here's what really happened." She told them about Hector da Silva and his money problems.

"Hector couldn't stand to lose the cruise line completely, though," Nancy continued. "He stayed on as general manager of the *Emerald Queen.* I think that even then he was still hoping that someday he'd be able to come up with the money to buy back the line from the new owners.

"So when a bright young crewman named Randy Wolfe suggested a foolproof way to steal a consignment of cut emeralds and sell them on the black market, Hector couldn't resist. Randy would hijack the consignment and deliver it to Hector."

"But wait a minute, Nancy," interrupted Carson Drew. "How did Antonio Ribeiro get in on all this? If I remember right, he was your number-one suspect all along."

"I'll get there, Dad," Nancy said with a twinkle. "Anyway, all Hector had to do then was hide the gems on the *Emerald Queen* and then notify the buyer in Miami. He wouldn't have to do any of the dirty work, and yet he'd end up millions of dollars richer."

Nancy took a sip of her orange juice. "My guess is that Antonio Ribeiro somehow found out about the whole plan." She looked at her father. "Remember when Mrs. da Silva said that Hector and Ribeiro got very friendly around that time? Well, it wasn't really a friendship—

Ribeiro was trying to blackmail Hector da Silva into sharing the wealth."

Carson Drew nodded. "I see."

Nancy went on with her story. "By this time, Randy had gone to Europe, and Hector didn't know what to do. He wasn't a natural criminal, so rather than do what Randy might have done —that is, kill Ribeiro—Hector simply changed the hiding place of the emeralds, and then notified Randy by letter that they were in a new place."

"Hold on a minute," Matt broke in, his face lined with confusion. "I'm lost. If Randy was in Europe, how could he be stealing emeralds in South America?"

"That was something that really threw me at first, too," Nancy confessed. "Until the very end, I assumed that Randy couldn't have had anything to do with the emerald thefts, because he was in Europe around the time they happened. But he slipped up when he lied and told me he'd never worked aboard the *Emerald Queen* before. Then, when I found out that he had, I wondered why he'd lied about it."

"Obviously," Ned put in, "Randy didn't want you to think he had any connection with da Silva."

"Right," Nancy said. "Actually, he left right *after* the emeralds were stolen—I'll bet that the records would prove that he left the morning the theft was discovered. When he first came up with his plan, he gave himself an alibi in advance by asking to be transferred to Europe. He could wait to collect his share of the profits until after the investigation trail cooled off."

"I think I see where you're going," Ned said excitedly. "Hector couldn't just tell Randy right out where the emeralds were hidden. You said that Hector was being investigated in connection with the theft, right? So his mail was probably under surveillance—he had to put everything in code."

"Smart boy!" Nancy squeezed Ned's hand under the table. "You're right again.

"Hector was really into codes, according to Mrs. da Silva. He wrote this letter to Randy, letting him know about the change of plans in some subtle way, and tried to convey the key to decoding the drawing that he had made. That letter, by the way, caused me major confusion—Randy had given a copy to Ribeiro, and that night when I asked you to cover for me, Melissa, I found it in Ribeiro's room. Since it was addressed to *R,* I assumed that Hector had written it to Ribeiro. It never occurred to me to wonder why Ribeiro would have a copy of the letter instead of the original."

"But why didn't Hector just send Randy the spider drawing?" asked Melissa. "It sure would have made things a lot simpler."

Nancy nodded. "Right—but he didn't want

them to be simple. He didn't trust Randy a hundred percent, and he wanted to be sure Nina got her fair share. So what he actually sent was a code of a code. It was the only way he could ensure Randy's cooperation.

"Anyway. Besides not having the drawing to tell him where to find the jewels, Randy Wolfe now had another problem on his hands. Ribeiro.

"Antonio Ribeiro hadn't forgotten about the emeralds, so when Randy came back, Ribeiro threatened to expose him unless Randy cut him in."

Ned interrupted. "Nancy, something doesn't make sense here. Randy Wolfe is a natural-born killer. Why not just get rid of Ribeiro?"

Nancy shook her head. "Randy is very smart. When he found out he had a new—and unwelcome—partner, he decided to let Ribeiro do all the dirty work. Ribeiro could take care of Mrs. da Silva once Randy got the map. And Randy made sure Ribeiro left a trail that would lead the police right to Ribeiro—but not to Randy himself. It was a perfect plan. Ribeiro would get the spider code from Mrs. da Silva, and Randy would get rid of *him*—after they got the jewels."

"Incredible. And because of various coincidences," Carson Drew began, "like your overhearing Ribeiro's conversation with Nina, and your finding that letter addressed to *R* in *Ribeiro's* cabin, and Nina herself thinking that Ribeiro was the one who had planned it all—"

"I never even thought of the possibility that the main brain in this case could have been anyone else," Nancy finished up. She gave a rueful laugh. "It should have been obvious. Such a lot of strange little facts didn't add up. But Ribeiro was so easy to spot that I didn't bother to look any further than that."

"You still haven't explained how you, Ned, and Randy ended up battling in a cable car thousands of feet up in the air," Matt pointed out.

Nancy grinned. "I'll let Ned tell you about that," she replied. "He was the hero!"

"Well—" Ned looked a little embarrassed. "As I was telling Nancy, Ribeiro came back to the *Emerald Queen* with another guy after he'd chased us off. I was hiding nearby, and I managed to overhear a lot of their conversation.

"Ribeiro wanted to grab as many of the emeralds as he could and take off before they got caught. But the other guy—who I later found out was Randy Wolfe—was much cooler. He was saying that all they had to do was take care of the two kids—meaning Nancy and me—and then lie low until the ship docked in Miami. Then they could just sell the gems, sit back, and enjoy being rich.

"But by then Ribeiro was really rattled. He

kept saying it was too risky, and he didn't want to risk a murder rap in Rio. I gather the police here can be pretty tough. So finally Randy said that he knew where Nancy and I might be going, and that he'd take care of us himself."

Melissa gasped. "How cold-blooded! What did you do?"

"The only thing I could," Ned answered simply. "Nancy's life was more important than the emeralds. So I waited until Ribeiro and Randy were gone, and then headed over to Sugarloaf as fast as I could go. And I was almost too late," he added, his face grim. "Randy and Nancy were in the cable car already—it was taking off and I just barely managed to jump on the roof."

Nancy leaned over and gave Ned a huge hug. "As usual, Nickerson, you did exactly the right thing. If you hadn't been there, I probably never would have made it to the top alive!" She shivered.

"What a mind!" Melissa said. "To think Randy had that whole plan worked out so carefully."

"Yes," Nancy agreed. "Randy is a brilliant criminal. If it hadn't been for a couple of unforeseeable hitches, he would have pulled it all off."

"But he's so young and—and handsome!" Melissa wailed. Matt gave her a shocked look and everybody laughed.

"Melissa, you sound just like a friend of mine back in River Heights," Nancy said. "Speaking of whom, I promised a lot of people I'd bring back some colorful pictures of life in fabulous Rio. Ned, do you have your camera with you?"

"Right here," Ned answered, holding it up.

"Great. What do you say we start working on a photo essay—right now, on the beach?"

"Let's go. See you later, everyone!"

As Ned and Nancy walked down the steps to the beach, Ned put his arm around Nancy's shoulders. "Hey, Nan?" he asked.

"Hmmmm?"

"I didn't think Randy was really that good-looking. Did you?"

Nancy stared at Ned in astonishment. Then she began to laugh. "He's not even in your league," she said.

"Positive?" Ned looked relieved.

"Definitely. There's *no* one in your league, Ned. Now, kiss me, you fool."

As Ned's arms slid around her waist, Nancy melted against him with a happy sigh. Romantic Rio with the guy she loved. What more could she want?

**Nancy's next case:**

Nancy is urgently summoned to Washington, D.C., by her old friend Senator Marilyn Kilpatrick. When Nancy arrives on Capitol Hill, the senator—fearing that her office is bugged—escorts Nancy to the street to talk. It seems that gossip columnist Beverly Bishop is about to publish a nasty exposé that will ruin lives, including Senator Kilpatrick's.

When Nancy visits the gossip columnist, she realizes that Beverly will stop at nothing to get her treacherous book into print, no matter who gets hurt. But will one of Beverly's intended victims try to get back at her? And can Nancy persuade Beverly not to write the final, poisonous chapter? Find out in *PURE POISON,* Case #29 in The Nancy Drew Files™.

Forthcoming Titles in the
Nancy Drew Files™ Series

No. 29 Pure Poison
No. 30 Death by Design
No. 31 Trouble in Tahiti
No. 32 High Marks For Malice
No. 33 Danger in Disguise
No. 34 Vanishing Act
No. 35 Bad Medicine
No. 36 Over The Edge

Simon & Schuster publish a wide range of titles from pre-school books to books for adults.

For up-to-date catalogues, please contact:

International Book Distributors
Campus 400
Maylands Avenue
Hemel Hempstead
Herts
HP2 7EZ

Tel. 0442 882255